ROAD KILL

COLIN M. ANDREWS

Published by New Generation Publishing in 2025

First Edition

Print ISBN: 9781835637616

New Generation Publishing
www.newgeneration-publishing.com

AUTHOR'S NOTES

The initial inspiration for this novel came from seeing a TV adaptation of Agatha Christie's 'Why Didn't They Ask Evans' – a whispered comment from a dying man!

The towns and villages in East Devon mentioned in this work of fiction are real, as are the pubs, and although the Rolle Arms in East Budleigh has been permanently closed for a long time it still has the name on the building. I've tried not to embarrass any residents by identifying too closely the abodes of the main characters, and in a few cases I've used some leeway in describing locations. All characters are fictional and no relation to any real person is intended. The investigating officer, D.I. Matthews, also featured in my previous novel, Captured Image.

The Inter-Varsity Folk Dance Festival referred to has been going for a good many years. I remember taking part as a member of Cardiff University Welsh Folk Dance Group at a festival in Hull back in the late sixties, and I've also participated in some events on at least one occasion when the festival has been held at Exeter University. The ceilidh band mentioned did actually perform at one such event.

Woodbury Castle is an amazing Iron Age hill fort on Woodbury Common between Ottery St Mary and Budleigh Salterton with views over the Exe estuary.

I'd like to thank Andy Richardson for proof reading and correcting any errors with reference to police procedure, and to my good friends, Susie Golightly and Anne Bendix, for general comments on the first draft. I take full responsibility for any remaining errors! Rather than use a photograph which would specifically identify a location for the initial incident, Jon Shapley kindly agreed to provide a front cover illustration based on my description. Thanks also to the team at New Generation for transforming the manuscript into a published book.

PROLOGUE

Mike Brooks enjoyed the freedom of the countryside. Especially on a clear summer morning like today when he could rise soon after dawn and cycle along the spider's web network of lanes around his village. He appreciated the choice of circular routes of varying distance that he could take, depending on how energetic he was feeling – or what the weather was doing. Rarely would he encounter any other person or vehicle.

Since retiring several years ago, he'd become very familiar with the lanes and byways, cycling or walking with his wife, Freda. Four years ago, however, Freda had been diagnosed with Alzheimer's, and as her dementia had worsened he had rarely left their cottage except for the hour or so when her care worker visited. Then, just over twelve months ago, she had fallen and sustained severe head injuries from which she never recovered. Though most distressing at the time, Mike's sorrow had given way to relief at being able once more to experience the peace and tranquility of the open country.

He did not immediately take much notice of the dark brown bundle as he pedalled past the field entrance. It wouldn't be the first time he'd come across a sack of rubbish dumped by the roadside by a fly-tipper who couldn't be bothered to take his junk to the local council recycling centre. Something, however, triggered curiosity in Mike's mind and he dismounted to go back for a closer look.

"Christ Almighty!" he muttered as he drew in his breath at the sight of a man's body curled up in the gateway.

CHAPTER 1

A month earlier

Miriam Roseberry drew back her bedroom curtain. The battered minibus which had pulled up across the road discharged its usual load of gaunt-looking men, mostly bearded, dark-skinned and shabbily dressed in jeans and sweater, with a beanie covering their head.

Miriam pursed her lips. She had witnessed the same scene almost every morning since the work on a new housing development had begun several weeks earlier. Her objections to the planning permission had been to no avail. When she had semi-retired to Topsham after leaving her shop in the hands of a manager, she had enjoyed the view over open fields and the peace and quiet of the location. Barely eighteen months later bulldozers and diggers had churned the idyllic landscape into a muddy tracks and huge piles of earth, and she had to live with the constant noise of heavy machinery. Already much of the green belt on Exeter's former eastern and southern boundaries had been extensively plastered with new houses and it was evident that Topsham was destined for the same fate.

That was bad enough, in her opinion, but the import of cheap foreign labour was for her the last straw. Probably illegal immigrants, made to work for next to nothing and shacked up in a barn. She'd certainly heard them gabbling in a strange language. She had initially reported her concerns to the police, who assured her that they would look into the matter, but had evidently given it very low priority since nothing seemed to have changed. They probably regarded her as some old bat with an aversion to any change and anything foreign. She had tried speaking to someone who she assumed was the foreman – or gangmaster, as she'd read in the newspaper, about similar building developments elsewhere – and she was told in no uncertain terms to f... off and mind her own business.

Well, if the police weren't prepared to act, she wasn't prepared to turn her back on the issue. She picked up the small business card she'd found in the newsagents and dialed the number.

CHAPTER 2

3 weeks earlier

Responding to brawls in town and city centre pubs was a regular part of the late shift for an Exmouth patrol car, particularly at weekends. To be called to such an event at a normally peaceful village pub, however, was a very rare event.

When the patrol officers entered the Rolle Arms in East Budleigh two men were going at each other hammer and tongs. After pulling them apart, they quickly scanned the public bar for witnesses as to what had led to the affray. Surprisingly, even for ten o'clock on a Friday evening, there were very few people in the pub – just a couple of old fellows in the corner nursing their half-finished pint and keeping their heads down, obviously not wanting to get involved. Quite possibly other customers had left as soon as the fighting had started. Cowering in a doorway behind the bar a young woman was keeping as far from the action as possible.

"Right, now what's this all about?" asked the Police Sergeant.

"This tosser accused me of stealing his girl-friend," replied a stocky round-faced man. His left eye socket was already discoloured and by the morning it would be a proper shiner.

"And you are?"

"Dennis Inwood. I'm the landlord."

"And a bloody lecherous bastard!" growled the other man between cut lips.

Inwood made to lunge again but was held back by the constable. "Comes in here pissed as a newt and starts effing and blinding about me sleeping with his woman."

"Any truth in that?"

"No. I've never touched her. "

"So you do know her?"

"She works here." he gestured with his thumb towards the barmaid. "You can ask her. I didn't know she had anything to do with this bloke."

"I suggest you get back behind the bar," the officer said to Inwood, then turned his attention to his accuser "Your name, sir?"

"Robert Paisley." His eyes followed Inwood as he walked away.

The sergeant took statements from Paisley and Inwood while his colleague spoke to the barmaid and the elderly customers.

"Do you wish to press charges?" the sergeant asked the landlord.

"No, but he'd better not set foot in this pub ever again."

CHAPTER 3

Saturday morning

The top of the man's head was blooded from a gash on his left temple. Mike's immediate impression was that he was looking at a corpse but his first aider training automatically kicked in and he knelt down to check for a pulse on the man's wrist. Surprisingly the hand was not stone cold and he thought he could detect a weak response. As he leaned closer to check the pulse again on the man's neck the body gave a brief shudder and the man's lips began to move. Mike put his ear to the man's mouth.

"Ce ... celia .. t... tell ..." came a whisper. Then nothing.

Mike took off his coat and laid it over the upper body, in the chance that it might just keep him warm enough to survive until help arrived. With coverage by most mobile phone networks notably unreliable in this part of Devon, Mike was relieved when his phone displayed one bar albeit intermittently, but it would no doubt allow an emergency call.

He dialled 999 and responded urgently to the operator's reply.

"Ambulance, please. I've found a man badly injured by the roadside. He's still alive but very weak. Also police, as he may be the victim of a hit and run." He paused while the operator requested further details. "My name is Michael Brooks. I'm just outside the village of East Budleigh, a right turn off Hayes Lane – that's opposite the Sir Walter Raleigh pub". Another pause. "Yes, of course I'll wait here. I don't think my mobile number will be of much use to contact me, though, as the signal is poor."

Mike looked at the man lying on the ground. He considered trying to move him into a recovery position, but he was already lying on his right side and his face was clear of the mud. He was dressed in faded jeans, and a dark green roll neck sweater. A brown loafer lay beside his left foot, the other still on his right foot. Not the kind of shoes for walking country lanes, Mike thought. He considered searching his pockets for some kind of identification but thought that the police would rather he left that task to to them.

He glanced at his watch. Gone 6.30 am He'd already been waiting nearly twenty minutes but the ambulance and police would presumably be coming from Exmouth. At least there was no-one at home this weekend who would be worried if he didn't get back for breakfast. Hopefully the police wouldn't keep him too long once they arrived. He'd take the shortest route back home to Otterton rather than complete the longer circular route he'd planned.

He caught sight of blue flashing lights of the ambulance coming up the road he had travelled just as a police car arrived from the opposite direction. While two paramedics attended the victim, a stocky middle-aged officer with a thin trimmed beard introduced himself as Sergeant Fentham and his colleague, a slim young woman, as P.C. Evans. "You found the gentlemen here and called it in?"

"Yes that's right."

"Seems very early for you to be out and about,"

"It's my regular exercise. A few miles cycling before the roads get busy with tractors or grockels. Very rarely see anybody about at all."

"And nobody this morning? No vehicles passing you?"

"None at all."

The sergeant turned as the paramedics approached, shaking his head. "I'm sorry, but I think this chap is beyond help."

"He's dead?" said the Sergeant in surprise.

"'Fraid so. We've tried to revive him but we were too late to save him."

Sergeant Fentham turned to Mike, "He was alive when you found him, er, Mr Brooks, is that correct?"

"Mike Brooks. Yes he was."

"You're sure about that?"

"Yes, I checked his pulse. I'm a first aider. If

he'd been dead I wouldn't have called for an ambulance."

"I understand you asked for the police as well?"

"Yes, it looked like a hit and run."

"You're probably right. We would have attended anyway given the circumstances."

P.C. Evans had just returned from looking at the body with the other medic and heard the last exchange. "Sarge, I think there might be a problem. From the state of his shoes it doesn't look as if he was walking these lanes."

"What?" After examining the footwear Sgt. Fentham then searched the pockets on the victim's jeans and shirt and Mike's coat. "I'm inclined to agree with you, clean shoes and no identification on the body whatsoever is cause for concern." He turned to Mike Brooks. "Did you take anything from the pockets?"

"Not at all. By the way that is my coat on his body. I put it over him to keep in body heat. Unnecessarily, so it seems. Can I have it back?"

Sgt Fentham stroked his beard, "Um, I'm not sure. I'm going to have to call this in for further investigation and I think it would probably be better for the scene to remain as I found it. If you would like to give your address and contact details to my colleague, we will get it back to you as soon as possible."

"Can I go back home then?"

"Yes, but you will be required to give a formal statement."

CHAPTER 4

As soon as he had been briefed, Detective Inspector Des Matthews relieved the officers who had originally responded to the emergency call. They had just received a call to attend a vehicle on fire at Woodbury Castle. The paramedics had long been dismissed, leaving the body for the attention of the police and the coroner.

"What do you make of this, Rachel?" said D.I. Matthews to his junior colleague, Detective Sergeant Rachel Allen, as they stepped back from the corpse and awaited the arrival of the forensic pathologist.

"Well, sir, it certainly doesn't appear to be a straightforward hit and run. Doesn't look like he was out for a morning stroll. And who in their right mind would go out without their mobile phone, house keys and wallet?"

"I agree. He's suffered a severe blow to the head, which probably killed him, but the bloke who found him was sure he was alive then.

"I suppose he could have been dumped here."

"Possible. From the tyre marks in the mud it certainly looks as if a vehicle stopped here recently and then pulled away. Bicycle tracks, too."

"Well, the chap who found the body was riding a bike, so we were told."

"True. It's evident that somehow, our victim's head made contact with that boulder. It's got a lot of blood on it, and I'm sure you noticed the abrasions on his face, as if someone had scratched his face with their fingernails. As you might do if you were attacked."

"I'd be much more likely to give him my knee in his bollocks!"

"Well, we'll find out whether he had any other injuries after Dr. Wilson has examined him," D.I. Matthews nodded towards the lanky man who had just extricated himself from the passenger seat of an almost impossibly small saloon car and was pulling on a white protective overall.

"Good morning to you, Des, and to you too, Rachel," Dr Wilson greeted them, "Sorry for the delay. My car wouldn't start so I've had to rely on my assistant, Brenda. Don't think you've met her before, she's only recently joined my team."

"Hi Brenda," D.I. Matthews nodded to her, "Right, Barry, we've got a body here for you to look at." Matthews raised the police cordon tape for him and stood by as Dr Wilson made an initial examination.

"He's certainly taken a nasty blow to his head, which could have been fatal. I can't say for certain until I've conducted the post mortem."

"Any idea how long he's been dead?"

"Quite recent, probably about an hour ago, but again I may be able to be more precise after I've examined him further."

"Okay, thanks. That tallies with what our witness said. I'll leave you to it now. Let me know as soon as possible what you find. We really need to identify him, so fingerprints, dental records, any evidence of surgery will be helpful."

"No I.D. on him?"

"Nothing at all."

"Odd."

* * *

"Where to now, boss?" said Rachel as she drove back into the village of East Budleigh.

"Back to the station, I think. We will need to talk to this Mike Brooks but I'd like to have some background on him, and ideally an identity for our victim. I'd like you to set up a house to house enquiry around the village and any other dwellings on the route and connecting roads nearby to see if anyone heard or saw anything at that god-forsaken hour of the morning – car, walkers, whatever. Perhaps someone exercising their dog early. It's probably too much to expect any CCTV out here but it might be worth checking on any vehicles heading this way from the nearest monitors."

"I'll get on to it, sir."

"Oh, and follow up reports on that burning vehicle at Woodbury Castle. It may not be related to this incident but we can't rule anything out at this stage. Then go home and enjoy the rest of your weekend. We'll meet first thing on Monday."

Matthews thought it unlikely that he'd be getting much relaxation over the weekend. Since transferring to Exmouth police station from Exeter earlier in the year after the break-up of his marriage and the need to find somewhere else to live, he'd chosen to spend as little time as possible in his sparsely furnished and rather dingy rented flat, sometimes even kipping overnight in his office. He'd always given his work priority over family life, as his ex-wife had frequently reminded him, so he resigned himself to the fact that she had wanted to opt out and seek a fresh start. Fortunately they had no children – another reason for her complaint, though they had tried, with the problem eventually diagnosed as due to his abnormally low sperm count. They had parted on amicable terms and he hoped that, still to reach forty years of age, she would find a more attentive – and fertile – partner with whom she could become a mother. Strictly on a professional basis, Matthews enjoyed the company of his new colleague, Rachel Allen, a vibrant and attractive young brunette some twelve years younger than him. She was in a steady relationship with a lad she'd known since her college days, and who apparently was a potential high-flier as an accountant in his father's firm. Whereas Matthews' former colleague at Middlemoor Police HQ, D.S.

Bob Nicholls, had been conscientious but rather reserved, Rachel was like a breath of fresh air, hard-working and very much on the ball.

CHAPTER 5

By late Monday morning, a probable identity for the victim had been established. Fingerprints had matched those of a Robert Paisley who had been convicted of assault as a teenager some twenty years earlier. He'd been given a suspended prison sentence. No further offences were on record. The burnt-out vehicle had also been identified as a Volkswagen Estate, with ten possible owners, including Robert Paisley, in the Exeter and East Devon area. Although the number plate was unreadable, the engine and chassis registration numbers were still being checked. The results of the post-mortem and dental checks were still awaited.

"It seems that Robert Paisley is a local lad," said Matthews to Rachel, who had just come off the telephone.

"In that case it is probable that he went to Exmouth School. I've just found out that Mike Brooks was a teacher there for many years, so he may well have known Paisley."

"Really? Then why didn't he identify the body?"

"Perhaps he wasn't asked. I don't think we raised the question, and I'm sure the attending officers would have told us."

"Hmm, in retrospect, an oversight. Top priority now is to speak to Brooks. Give him a ring, will you and tell him we're on our way." Matthews thought for a moment. "And just check on the DVLA address we've got in Paisley's name for an VW Estate."

* * *

Mike Brooks had opened the front door of his modern semi even before they had knocked. "Inspector Matthews? Do come in. I've been expecting you."

Matthews regarded the tall gent standing before him, casually dressed in grey slacks and green unbuttoned cardigan over a cream round-necked t-shirt. Though retired, he'd aged well, with the face free of wrinkles and lines, and still a trace of sandy colour in his thick mop of white hair.

"Thank you for agreeing to talk to us," He introduced Rachel, "This my colleague, D.S. Allen."

Mike led them through the hallway into the dining room at the rear. "Please take a seat. It's warmer in here. Cup of tea? Coffee?"

"Thank you, but not for us," Matthews answered for both of them. "Now, I know you have already given a statement to the other officers at the scene, but it would be helpful if you could just take us through the events again."

"No problem. I was out for my early morning

ride. I usually do a round trip of up to twelve miles, depending on the weather, and going through East Budleigh gives me several options.

"What time did you leave home?" Matthews interjected.

"Oh, about five-thirty I suppose."

"So you would have got to the scene by, say, six o'clock?"

"Er, yes. I heard the church clock strike as I was cycling along the lane opposite the pub."

"Go on!"

"I turned right to take the road up to join the one from Yettington to Bicton Arena. It was along there that I saw the body lying by the field gateway. I thought he was dead."

"But he wasn't?"

"No, I thought I could detect a pulse. And he spoke to me."

"What?" Matthews' eyebrows shot skywards, and D.S. Allen glanced at her boss with a frown.

"What did he say?"

Mike thought for a moment. "His voice was very quiet, little more than a whisper. I think he said 'Tell Celia'."

"Why didn't you mention this before?" Matthews spoke sharply.

"I'm sorry. I thought I did. But I guess my mind wasn't very clear. It's not the sort of thing you expect to happen."

"Do you know anyone called Celia?" Rachel Allen interposed.

"No, sorry."

"Okay, let's move on," Matthews said, "Did you recognise the victim?"

"No, I didn't."

"Are you certain about that? You see, we are pretty sure we have identified him as Robert Paisley. He was a student at Exmouth School, where you were a teacher."

It was Mike's turn to show surprise. "Christ, that's a long time ago – before I retired, Must be at least twenty years."

"You recognise the name?"

"Yes, indeed, though he's changed a lot over the years and I certainly didn't recognise him." Mike reflected for a moment. "He was a pain in the ass. Very cocky and self-assured. Always trying to wind up teachers who showed any weakness in the classroom."

"Did he wind you up?"

"He tried, once."

"What did you do to prevent further trouble? Report him?"

"No. I had a private meeting with him in which he got the message that it was not in his interest to mess about with me in the classroom."

"I would imagine he wasn't very happy with you," said D.S. Allen.

"Well, he wasn't in my fan club but it's difficult to know whether he bore me any animosity or just showed grudging respect for having the balls to stand up to him."

"And you haven't seen him since?"

"No. I vaguely recall hearing that he'd joined the army but whether he's still in the forces I don't know."

"Was there any student called Celia at school as the same time as Paisley?"

"Not that I personally recall, but it's always been a large school and I couldn't say for certain that there wasn't a Celia amongst the twelve hundred or so kids."

"How long have you been retired?" Matthews asked.

"Fifteen years this summer."

"You don't look that old," Allen commented.

"Thank you. No, I'm not. Just turned sixty-five. There was the opportunity to take early retirement which I was pleased to accept. No regrets at all on that decision."

Matthews looked at his colleague, and stood up. "Well, thank you, Mr Brooks, for your time, that's all for now." He gave Mike a card. "If you think of anything else that has slipped your mind please let me know."

Outside the house Matthews asked Rachel for her impressions of Mike Brooks.

"Well, sir, he seemed to be pretty straightforward and relaxed with his answers."

"Do you think he was telling the truth?"

Rachel shrugged, "Probably, I can't think of any reason why he would need to lie or withhold information. What about you, sir?"

"Hmm, on the face of it I've no cause to suspect otherwise but I have that niggling feeling that he might be holding something back. I'd like you to do a follow up check on him with the school to find out exactly when Paisley was there, and whether there is anything else about either of them relevant to this investigation."

"Will do."

"Also, has there been any feedback from house to house enquiries in the East Budleigh area?"

"Nothing very much. Just as he was getting up, a farmer about half a mile from the scene heard a car passing at speed."

"Time? Direction?"

"Five-thirty ish. And away from the scene past the farm."

"Anything else?"

"One old woman thought she saw someone pedalling along Hayes Lane early that morning but she can't be sure of the time, and whether it was a man or a woman."

"So it could have been Brooks?"

"That seems likely."

CHAPTER 6

A visit to Robert Paisley's address, provided by the DVLA as one of the registered owners of a VW Estate, was high priority on Matthew's agenda for the investigation into his death. However, as parking in Bicton Street was always difficult, he decided to return to the police station, which was only a short walk distant. They could also grab a quick sandwich and coffee and check for any updates.

Matthews had barely entered his office when the pathologist phoned.

"Hi, Des, Barry here. Thought you'd want to know what I've found out about your roadside corpse. White male, late thirties, possibly early forties. Quite a heavy drinker going by the state of his liver, and he would have had a skinful a few hours before his death."

"Can you confirm time of death?"

"Probably between six and six-thirty in the morning."

"And the cause?"

"Primarily the head injury. His head must have

struck the boulder quite forcibly. Consistent with having struck it from some height. Death would not necessarily have been instantaneous but it caused internal bleeding in the skull, which would have proved fatal."

"So the body being flung in the air from a hit and run is likely?"

"Ye .. yes," Barry Wilson paused, " but strangely there were no injuries to his lower body which I would have expected had he been struck by a vehicle while walking. "

"I see. Could his body have been thrown by, say, two people holding him."

"Possibly."

"How much time do you think would have passed between sustaining the injury and dying?"

"Not more than about half an hour, one hour at the outside."

"Anything else of significance?"

"He had multiple abrasions – very recently inflicted – on his face, which you probably noticed anyway. Probably sharp finer nails or possibly a cat's claws. And there were some fibre fragments in his nose, matching those of the coat which covered his body."

"Significant do you think? The person who found the victim did say he'd covered him with his coat?"

"I've no cause for suspicion."

"Okay, Barry, many thanks for giving it your prompt attention."

"No problem. I'll send the full written report over to you."

Robert Paisley's first floor flat was in the middle of a one-way residential street close to the town centre with, as expected, cars parked nose to tail on one side, and double yellow lines on the other, leaving just about enough width for vehicles to drive down. Fortunately Rachel Allen had been able to track down the landlord and obtain a spare key. However, when they arrived the door was already open.

"Looks as if it's been forced," said Matthews.

The flat was functional but small. A lounge-cum-dining room overlooked the street, while at the rear the double bed, set hard against the wall, took up most of the space in the bedroom, with just enough access for a small built-in wardrobe in an alcove and a cheap well-worn desk and chair beneath the window. A kitchenette with sink, stove and upright fridge-freezer, and a basic toilet, washbasin and shower completed the facilities. It was very much a bachelor's pad, spartan, with nothing for decoration other than a picture of a haggard-looking terrier hanging skew-whiff above the mantelpiece at a bricked-up fireplace, in front of which stood an electric radiator. It was obvious that someone had been searching the flat as all the drawers and cupboards were hanging open, with clothes and papers scattered everywhere.

Matthews took out his mobile phone. "We'll

take a look around but I'm calling this in as a crime scene."

Rachel commented on the open lap-top dumped beside the desk. "Wonder why this wasn't taken."

"Perhaps the intruder was disturbed – or was looking for something else, like cash. Anyhow, we'll take it to see if it contains anything useful."

"No family photographs, either," said Rachel, "In fact no photos at all."

"Not surprising, I suppose. We haven't yet been able to trace any family."

Their search of the flat took barely fifteen minutes, yielding only a few bills and receipts. On a final scan around the bathroom, Rachel pressed the pedal of the waste bin and called out "Sir, come and look at this!"

In the bin were a couple of bloodstained paper handkerchiefs.

Matthews shrugged his shoulders. "Well, he could just have had a nosebleed but forensics can find out if it is Paisley's blood and whether there are any other traces of blood in the flat that might suggest foul play. They will be testing for fingerprints too. We might get lucky and find a match on our system for whoever broke in. I've asked the station to send a uniform down here to stand guard on the door till they arrive."

"Will do. Er, then what are we doing, sir?"

"Pay a visit to the pub at the end of this road. If Paisley was a heavy drinker then it's quite probable it was his local boozer. See if they recognise him, at least."

Although the Bicton Inn stayed open all afternoon, there were only a couple of elderly men at a table nursing half a pint, while the barman, a swarthy fellow with a shaved head and dark stubble, was engrossed with a newspaper, pen poised above a crossword – or to pick a winner from the runners at day's races. He looked up as the unfamiliar couple approached.

"Good afternoon, sir and madam. What can I get you?"

"I'm D.I. Matthews and this is D.S. Allen," said Matthews, as they held up their warrant cards. "We are wondering whether you can identify this man." Matthews showed the barman a photo on his mobile phone. "We think he might be one of your regulars."

The barman squinted at the phone. "Yes, that looks like Robert Paisley. Lives just up the road. What's he done?"

"I'm afraid that we are investigating his death," said Matthews, pocketing his phone. "His body was found early on Saturday morning."

"Really? Where?" The barman didn't seem too concerned about the news.

"Near East Budleigh. When was the last time you saw him?"

"Probably here on Friday evening."

"Any idea what time he left?"

"Dunno. We were very busy." The landlord

paused for a moment. "No, hang on, that must have been Thursday. He wasn't here because I remember two blokes came in on Friday evening asking about him."

"Can you describe them?"

"Christ, Let me think! Both strong arm types, shaven headed. Neither local. One probably a Londoner and the other had a foreign accent."

"Would you recognise them again?"

"Doubtful, I only gave them a glance to tell them Paisley wasn't here."

"Is there anything you can tell us about him? His friends? Where he worked?"

"Not really. He was a regular here but never chatted to me much – he seemed a bit of a loner. Though there are a couple of blokes he used to drink with. They'll be in this evening, no doubt. They might be able to tell you more about him."

"Thanks very much for your help."

"Are you sure I can't pull you a pint or a wine for your young lady? On the house."

"Thank you, but no. I'll save it until this evening." Behind him Rachel barely suppressed a giggle.

As they walked back towards Paisley's flat, Rachel couldn't resist asking, "Are you going to take him up on that free pint this evening, sir?"

"I doubt if he'll want to give a free pint to a copper in front of a bar full of his regular customers, but I will go back there to see if I can get any more background on Paisley from his drinking buddies."

Matthews spoke briefly to the young police

constable standing outside the flat, "Are the team still inside?"

"Yes, sir, they only arrived a few minutes ago."

"Okay, then, we'll take over. You can go back to your normal duties."

"Thank you, sir."

CHAPTER 7

Tuesday

Matthews had arrived at the station early, hoping to spend some time examining the content of Paisley's laptop, but he'd been called out when a body had been discovered washed up on the shore at Weston Beach. Although only a short distance as the crow flies from Sidmouth, the location was not easily accessible, certainly by road. It seemed a pretty pointless use of his time, Matthews thought, since there was little to suggest that the dead male, of likely Indian or Pakistani origin, had been the victim of any crime. Probably came to grief attempting illegal immigration in a rubber dinghy.

On returning to his office, his frustration increased when he found that he couldn't access the laptop, even with the help of a computer geek in the office. He'd have to send it away for the technical services lab to unlock or overcome the password.

The previous evening's return visit to the Bicton Arms had provided little extra information about

Paisley while confirming the fact that he was a loner with no real friends or family, and didn't have a steady girl friend. "Too much of a temper, particularly when he'd a had a few pints, for a girl to stay with him any length of time," one drinking companion had commented, "though I think he did mention a Celia." The drinker hadn't been able to give any definite time scale for a Celia relationship but believed it was sometime during the previous six months. Matthews' enquiry into Paisley's occupation was also vague. "He works alone," one had said, "something like a private eye. But he was in the army for a while."

Matthews brought his young colleague up to date with what he had found.

"If he was into private investigations, it's possible he may have seriously pissed someone off," Rachel commented.

"That's certainly one line of enquiry we need to follow up," said Matthews. "Hopefully the laptop may give us some clues. Have you got anything new for me?"

"Yes sir. I called at the school on my way in this morning. It seems Mike Brooks had a bit of a reputation."

"Oh yes?"

"His nickname was Basher Brooks. Seems he might have been rather free with his hands in disciplining errant pupils."

"So Paisley might have had a genuine grievance against him, and may have confronted him"

"After all this time, sir? You don't really think that Brooks could have had anything to do this Paisley's death?"

"Probably not but I'm ruling nothing out at the moment."

"There is another thing, sir. It seems that Brooks didn't just take early retirement. He was, shall we say, 'encouraged to leave'."

"Why?"

"There were allegations of indecently assaulting a young sixth form female student. Not proven, however, as the investigation was dropped when she failed to make a formal complaint, but Brooks' reputation was irreparably damaged."

"What was this student's name?"

"Leah Morgan."

"We need to have another word with our Mister Brooks. He hasn't been entirely forthcoming with us. And also, see if you can trace Leah Morgan. It will be interesting to hear her side of the story."

* * *

Mike Brooks was mowing his front lawn when he heard a vehicle pull up outside. He was surprised to see the two detectives get out of the car and approach him. "Oh, it's you again. I'm sorry I haven't remembered anything else." he said.

"There's one or two things we just need to check with you," replied Matthews, "May we come inside?"

"No problem." Mike disconnected the mower cable from the extension socket. "Go on in. You know where the living room is."

When they were seated and Matthews had again declined any refreshment, he began by asking what specialist subjects Mike taught.

"I was a physics specialist but in the lower school I also taught general science, so a bit of chemistry and biology." Mike replied amiably.

Matthews thought his next question would probably remove the friendly smile from his face. "When you were teaching did you ever use physical punishment on any of your pupils?"

Mike showed some surprise but remained calm, pausing only briefly before replying. "Occasionally. It wasn't unusual when I first started teaching."

"My colleague, D.S. Allen, made some enquiries at your old school, mainly to get some background on Robert Paisley, but also, in passing, to confirm the details you provided about yourself. It seems your nickname was Basher Brooks, which rather suggests you might have been a little more inclined to be physical with discipline."

"I assure you I wasn't. I've a pretty good idea who came up with that nickname. He wasn't a troublesome kid but very quick witted and often quite amusing with comments. That one, after I'd slapped his friend for swearing in class, wasn't funny but I was stuck with it ever after."

"Did you assault Robert Paisley in your private meeting?" Rachel Allen asked.

"No, but I did make him aware of the consequences if he persisted in deliberately irritating me."

"Which could have been a threat of physical violence?" she continued.

"No comment."

Matthews took up the questioning again. "What about your alleged assault on Leah Morgan?"

A flicker of a frown passed over Mike's face. "Unfounded. Leah was a compulsive flirt with anyone in trousers. She had a crush on me and didn't like it when I rejected her advances. It was her father who made the allegations but she denied any inappropriate action by me when it came to be investigated."

"You weren't made to leave?"

"Not in so many words. I had been suspended – briefly – until the investigation was terminated, but when the offer of early retirement was made, I felt I'd had enough. Particularly as the tick-box culture and rigid conformation to key stage targets had killed off any freedom we had previously enjoyed to sometimes diverge from the set syllabus. It was what made teaching enjoyable both for myself and my students. And single science GCSE subjects were being dumped in favour of general science, which personally I thought was very ill-advised."

Matthews got the impression that Brooks was getting in to soap-box speaker mode, and quickly brought the focus back to his investigation. "Have you been in touch with Leah since?"

"I think she still lives in this area, but, to answer your question, no."

"Just one more point, can you recall any school friends of Leah that may be able to corroborate your account?"

Mike thought for a few moments. "Possibly. There was a Candy Archer and a Pippa Hendricks, but I've absolutely no idea where they are now. Anyway, I can't see how this is relevant to the death of Robert Paisley."

"You're probably right, sir. It's just that in the police we still have to tick all the boxes."

The lanky young man flicked the mop of long fair hair from his face as he looked at the unfamiliar occupants of the car that had just passed him. He pedalled on for another hundred yards and dismounted outside the house where the car had recently been parked.

"Steven!" exclaimed Mike, as he stood up from reconnecting the lawn mower to the extension cable.

"Hi Dad," With his bike propped up against the wall and a grey rucksack dumped on the path, the young man greeted Mike with a hug.

"Surprised to see you midweek – and mid-afternoon."

"Ah well, I had a bit of free time."

"Pleased to see you anyway, Steven."

"Who were those blokes in the car? Not trying to sell you something?"

"No, a couple of detectives from Exmouth."

"What did they want?"

"Some follow up to the body I found on Saturday morning." Mike saw the look of surprise on his son's face. "Oh, of course you weren't here last weekend. Found this bloke by the roadside on my early morning ride."

"Not someone you knew I hope."

"Not that I recognised though apparently I taught him many years ago, when you would have been no more than a toddler."

Mike and his late wife, Freda, had their first son, Simon, within a year of getting married, and Steven was an unexpected addition to the family some ten years later when Freda had thought her menopause had already started. He had Mike's blonde hair and build but his features were very much modeled of those of his mother – a rounded face, brown eyes, and a small nose, slightly turned up at the end, unlike Mike's Roman conk. He'd always been rather shy and studious, and Mike was rather surprised when Steven had initially thought about becoming a teacher, albeit at Primary level. Mike would have been concerned that Steven might face some problems in controlling young teenagers like Paisley. As it happened even before he'd completed B.A. Degree, Steven had decided, like his brother, not to follow his father's profession.

"Can I stay the night, Dad?"

"Sure, no problem. Bed is still made up from the weekend." Mike thought for a moment. "No upset with your flat mate I hope? "

"No, not at all, but he's, um, entertaining this evening." Steven grinned. "And they say, three's a crowd."

"I get the message." Mike said. "No girlfriend for you, yet, then?"

"Nothing serious."

CHAPTER 8

Wednesday

No further items of information had been received until, like buses, three arrived almost simultaneously.

First of all, a Leah Morgan had been found on the electoral roll with an address in Budleigh Salterton. Her date of birth also put her within the correct age range for her to have been a student at Exmouth School shortly before Mike Brooks retired.

A query into Paisley's possible army career had produced a report that he had indeed served for twelve years from the age of eighteen, and was a corporal when he was discharged for assaulting a senior female officer while drunk on duty. Matthews was digesting this latest information when his sergeant tapped on his office door.

"Sir, I was looking through some logs over the past few weeks to see if Paisley had featured in any incidents."

"Go on."

"It seems the police were called to a fracas at a pub between Paisley and the landlord."

"Okay."

"And one of the officers attending the incident was P.C. Brooks."

"Oh really? Would that be any relation to Mike Brooks?

"His elder son, Simon."

"Okay, thanks, Rachel. I don't suppose he's in the station at the moment?"

"Actually he is."

"Please ask him to come up to my office."

When the young constable entered, Matthews could see in his face a resemblance to Mike Brooks. "I understand you were one of the officers attending an incident involving Robert Paisley."

"Yes sir, it was at the Rolle Arms."

"Were you aware that we are investigating the suspicious death of Paisley?"

Simon Brooks paused for a moment before replying, "I'd heard it mentioned around the station."

"Paisley had accused the landlord of stealing his girl-friend. Is that correct?"

"Yes, sir. Though the landlord denied it."

"Did you think he was telling the truth?"

"I think so, though one of the elderly men I spoke to in the pub told me that he had an eye for a pretty girl, and young barmaids often didn't stay more than a few weeks."

"What about the barmaid?"

"She told me that he had tried it on, but she made it clear she wasn't interested in him"

"Did you get her name? I see it isn't in the report."

"Er, yes, but as no charges were being brought my sarge didn't ask me for her name or those of the customers."

"And her name?"

"Celia Telling. She was the person who called the police."

Matthews glanced at Rachel Allen and gave her a thumbs up sign. "How did she seem to be reacting to the incident?

"Nervous I think. Very quiet and reserved."

"One last thing, were you aware that it was your father, Mike Brooks, who found Paisley's body?"

"No, I wasn't." Matthews felt that the denial came rather too quickly and without any surprise registering in the constable's face or tone.

"Your father hasn't discussed the incident with you?"

"No, sir. We meet up from time to time but not in the last couple of weeks."

After P.C. Brooks had been dismissed, Matthews sat back in his chair, hand behind his head, looking at the ceiling, clearly deep in thought. Rachel Allen waited quietly for further comments and instructions.

"Well, Rachel, it seems as if Mike Brooks wasn't imagining things in claiming he heard Paisley speak. From not knowing quite where to turn next we've now got at least three people to interview, and another possible suspect."

"Where do you want to start, sir?"

CHAPTER 9

Matthews doubted that there would be many lunchtime customers in the Rolle Arms, as the tourist season was not due to get seriously under way for another few weeks when the school summer term ended. Being on a main road to the relatively genteel seaside resort of Budleigh Salterton, it could expect to entice casual passers-by in the high season with its advertised carvery at weekends and special offers of standard pub fare during the week. Local people were less likely to seek lunchtime meals, and if they wished to dine out in the evening East Budleigh's quaint village pub, The Sir Walter Raleigh, would be more popular.

A young couple had dumped their rucksacks on the window seat in one corner of the pub and were engaged in seemingly intimate conversation. They took no notice of the arrival of Matthews and Allen. Neither did a more smartly dressed middle-aged gentlemen who sat alone at a table, scanning the financial pages of the Times and taking the occasional sup of his half pint of stout. Sitting at the far end of the bar three other well-built but swarthy men, dressed in clothes obviously suited for manual work, glanced at the new arrivals, their eyes lingering rather longer on Rachel's shapely figure before returning to conversation and their pint and sandwich.

The petite but attractive dark-haired girl behind the bar smiled at the new arrivals as they approached. Matthews guessed she was probably in her early thirties. No wedding ring,

"Good afternoon, sir and madam, what would you like to drink?"

"Just a coffee for me if it's not too much trouble." Matthews turned to his sergeant raising an eyebrow to indicate he was buying.

"An orange juice for me, thank you." Had they not been on duty Rachel would have preferred a large glass of Chardonnay.

"No problem."

When the barmaid brought their drinks over to their table, Matthews quietly asked "Are you Celia Telling?"

Though her eyes widened in surprise at the question, she nodded. Matthews discreetly showed her his warrant card. "We would like to have a word with you, and with Mr Inwood, if he is here." Seeing a look of concern in her face he added, "Nothing to worry about, just doing some follow up on an incident reported here a few weeks ago."

"I'll ask Mr Inwood to come out. He's probably in the kitchen."

A couple of minutes passed before a portly round-faced man emerged from the doorway behind the bar, followed by Celia. Looking at him, with his large white apron and white shirt, and, incongruously, a small hat, he reminded Rachel of Raymond Briggs' Snowman. His prominent reddened nose could well have been the carrot. Leaving Celia to tend to the bar, he waddled over to the detectives' table. "How can I help you, gentlemen?" His voice was surprisingly high pitched.

"Can we go somewhere private?" Matthews asked.

Inwood jerked his thumb, "Over in the corner there, or in my office if you prefer."

"Your office would be better."

Shrugging his shoulders, Inwood said, "Okay."

The detectives picked up their drinks and followed him. The office was little more than a large alcove beyond the kitchen. Apart from a chopping board with remnants of tomato and cucumber and a plastic bag half full of sliced white bread, there was little evidence of lunchtime food orders. Inwood indicated with his hand for Rachel to take the only chair, then perched himself on the edge of the old fashioned wooden desk.

Matthews remained standing. "We understand that the police were called to this pub a few weeks ago when a fight broke out between you and a customer."

"He wasn't a ruddy customer – and he certainly

won't be welcome as one while I'm here! Came in, already pretty pissed, and started ranting on about me stealing his girl-friend."

"That would be Celia, the barmaid?" Matthews interjected.

"Yes, but she's not my girl friend. She's my employee."

"We have heard that you are attracted to young women."

Inwood grinned, "Well, who wouldn't be?"

"Have you ever tried it on with Celia?"

"Not really. But she thought I was getting too close to her on one occasion and letting my hand stray. She slapped my face."

"She's still working here, though. You didn't sack her?"

"No, she apologised – and so did I. She's a hard worker and popular with the customers."

"Getting back to the fight, did you know your assailant?"

"Not by name. I think he may have been in the pub once or twice before."

"On his own?"

Inwood shrugged. "I really can't remember."

"And have you seen him since?"

Inwood hesitated. "Not in the pub, but a couple of weeks later we had closed for the evening, and Celia had just left by the main door. I was just about to lock up when I heard her cry out. I went outside, and saw that this same bloke had grabbed her. I pulled him off and punched him on the nose during the struggle. He slunk away cursing me and Celia, and mopping blood from his face."

"This wasn't reported?"

"Didn't really see the point. Er, why are you detectives taking an interest in this? I thought this was all sorted?"

"We are investigating the suspicious death of Robert Paisley. He is the person who threatened you. Celia was his former girlfriend."

"Bloody hell!"

"For the record, Mr Inwood, can you tell us where you were in the early hours of last Saturday morning?"

"After locking up, I was in bed by twelve thirty and slept through till about seven o'clock. And before you ask, I was on my own."

"And what kind of car do you drive?"

"It's a Citroen C3 Xsara. Quite big enough for my needs."

"Okay, sir, I think that's all for now. Perhaps you could relieve Celia at the bar so that we can talk to her – in here if that's okay with you."

Rachel stood up as Celia entered and offered her the only seat.

"Thank you. I've never sat in Dennis' chair before!" Celia looked nervously at both officers.

Matthews tried to put her at ease. "Please relax, Miss Telling. As I said earlier, we are here to clear up a few details, and hopefully find out a little more about Robert Paisley. You were his girl-friend, I believe?"

Celia nodded.

"And you called the police when he turned up at this pub and threatened Dennis?"

"Yes. I knew he had a violent temper, particularly when he'd been drinking, and he started lashing out."

"He was accusing Dennis of stealing you, his girl friend. Any truth in that?"

"No way! Dennis is a flirt but I made it very clear to him to keep his hands off me, and I'd already finished with Robert."

"How long were you with Robert before you ended the affair?"

"About five or six months. He was really kind and loving at first but within a few weeks he was getting abusive, particularly when he'd been drinking. Very demanding, and then he started using his fists on my body so the bruises wouldn't show. I became scared that it would get even worse and so I left him one weekend when I knew he was working away."

"What was he working at?"

"He told me he was a private investigator."

"And what kind of car did he drive?"

"He had a Volkswagen Estate when I was with him. He might have changed it since." Celia blinked quickly two or three times and said, "Has anything happened to him? Is that why you're here?"

"You didn't know he was found dead not far from here last Saturday morning? We are investigating the circumstances."

"No, I didn't. I had heard rumours of a hit and run accident but that's all." Celia looked down, her hands clasped tightly on her lap. "I'm – I'm not sorry he's dead, He was a good man at heart but I'm no longer going to be looking over my shoulder when I'm alone."

"Yes, we understand that can't have been easy for you," said Matthews. "Was the incident here in the pub the last time you saw him?"

"No, he was waiting outside one night after we had closed. If Dennis hadn't intervened it … it might have been my death you would be investigating."

"You really think so?"

"I don't know – dunno! I DON'T KNOW!" Tears were welling in her eyes.

Rachel bent down to calm her. "Okay love, calm down. He can't hurt you now anyway."

Matthews nodded at his sergeant, silently expressing his approval. "We're nearly done now, Celia. Just a couple more questions."

Celia grimaced.

"Were you living with Robert in Exmouth during the few months you were with him?"

Celia looked surprised. "No, we had a flat in Topsham."

"And where did you go when you left him? And when was that?"

"It was about six weeks ago. I went back to my mother's house at first. She lives in Crediton, but then she suggested I look after my aunt's old house here in East Budleigh until they've sorted out her will and my mother can sell it. It was left to her."

"Please let us have the address," said Matthews.

"So how long have you been working at this pub?" asked Rachel Allen.

"About five weeks – virtually ever since I moved in. I saw a notice advertising the vacancy the first time I came to the village."

"Easy walking distance then."

"Actually, I use my bike, Not keen on walking back on my own at night, certainly since Robert turned up again." Celia glanced towards the bar. "Are we finished?"

"Almost." Matthews paused, as if wondering whether to mention something or not. "The person who discovered Robert Paisley claimed that he was still alive and whispered 'Tell Celia'. Why do you think he would have mentioned your name in what was probably his last breath?"

Genuine surprise, eyebrows shooting upwards, showed on Celia's face. "What! Seriously?"

Matthews nodded.

"I've no idea. Small comfort I suppose that he was still thinking of me."

"Do you know Mike Brooks? He's the chap who found Robert."

"No, I don't." Celia shook her head.

"Or perhaps his son, Simon?"

"No, I don't think so." She looked puzzled.

"He was the policeman who answered your

emergency call about the fight."

"Oh, right. Yes, very polite young man."

"Just for the record, were you at home after finishing work on Friday?"

"Yes."

"You didn't see Robert?"

"No."

"Forgive me asking, but was anyone else at the house with you?"

Matthews thought he detected a slight hesitation before Celia replied, "No."

"No boy friend?"

"I'm not in a relationship."

Not quite a confirmation or denial, Matthews thought. "Well, that is all for now," he said. "Thank you for your time. It is possible that we may need to speak to you again, but in the meantime you can rest easy knowing that Robert Paisley won't be pestering you again." Another thought occurred just as he turned to leave. "Oh by the way, we haven't been able to trace any of his relatives. Would you be prepared to formally identify the body?"

Celia wrinkled her nose. "Must I? Surely there is someone else."

"Not that we know of. It would be very helpful."

"All right, I suppose so."

"All done, then?" said Dennis Inwood as the trio returned to the bar.

"Fine for now. Thanks." replied Matthews.

"Back to the station, sir?" said Rachel as they

walked to their car parked across the road.

"Not just yet. While we're here let's just have a look where Celia lives."

They drove up into the village and turned left opposite the Sir Walter Raleigh pub. Her cottage was close to the car park.

"Not all that far from here to where the body was found," Matthews commented.

"You surely don't think Celia could have dumped the body, sir? She'd have difficulty in shifting a full barrel of beer let alone a fellow the size of Paisley."

"No, you're right. Unless she had help. Inwood perhaps? Anyway it's all speculation until we get some firm evidence. And we've got another interview to do."

CHAPTER 10

It made sense to call on Leah Morgan on their way back to the Police Station as Budleigh Salterton was only a short distance from East Budleigh and only a slight deviation from their direct route to Exmouth. Whether they had the correct Leah Morgan and whether she would be at home on a Wednesday afternoon they would soon find out.

The house at the address they had obtained was one in a terrace of quite substantial properties in a residential cul-de-sac barely a mile from the town centre, which was effectively the main street leading down to the west end of the promenade. The small front garden was well tended, with a pocket size lawn and a selection of rose bushes.

Matthews parked behind a small red Suzuki Alto which displayed L plates.

"Rather more up-market than Paisley's place," Rachel commented as she opened the metal gate to let her boss through onto the path to the front door.

"True, but this would probably be towards the

lower end of the scale for property in Budleigh."

A few moments after pressing the bell, the door was opened by a slim woman casually, though nevertheless smartly dressed in pale green slacks with a light short-sleeved yellow cardigan over a cream blouse. Her blonde hair was neatly coiffured, barely reaching to her shoulders, perfectly suiting her round face and delicate features. A very attractive woman, Matthews thought, probably in her mid-thirties. In the passageway behind her, a young child peeked round a door.

"Leah Morgan?" Matthews asked gently.

"Yes, that's me." Her pleasant smile changed to a slight frown.

"I'm Detective Inspector Matthews and this is my colleague Detective Sergeant Allen." They both held up their warrant cards.

Alarm now showed on Leah's face. "Has something happened to Chris?" she cried.

"No, it's nothing to worry about. We are just checking up on the background of a key witness to a recent incident, and your name came up."

"Oh really?" Relief but surprise in Leah's voice.

"May we come inside and talk? We won't take much of your time."

"Er, yes, of course." She stood aside to let them enter then called to the child, "Stella, will you please go up to your room and play. I need to speak to these visitors."

"Okay, Mum." The young girl scrambled up the stairs, singing to herself.

"She seems a happy lass," said Rachel.

"She's a poppet." Leah led them into a tastefully furnished front lounge and invited them to take the sofa while she settled in an arm chair. "Now what is it you want to know?"

"We are looking at a possible hit and run incident. The victim was discovered by a Michael Brooks." Matthews noted her eyebrows shoot up at the mention of the name, confirmation, he thought, that they were talking to the right person.

"We discovered that Michael Brooks was a teacher at the school where our victim was a student. In the course of our investigation it also came to light that he was encouraged to take early retirement as a result of an allegation of sexual assault on a teenage girl – which was you, Leah Morgan. Is it true he assaulted you?"

"No, but I did fancy him."

"You didn't report him for assault?"

A look of annoyance passed over Leah's face. "That was my father's doing. He seemed convinced that Mike was a paedophile."

"Why did he do that?" D.S. Allen asked.

"God knows. Probably just to irritate me. He's always been a control freak. My mother divorced him when I was still at primary school and I lived mostly with her but used to stay with him every other weekend. He didn't like it when I started to show independence after I reached sixteen and his action against Mike Brooks was the last straw and I refused to have any more contact with him. My mother has since remarried."

"Is your father still around?"

"Yes. He's a builder, Charles Morgan. You may have come across him."

"Not that I recall."

"As I said, I have as little to do with him as possible. Give him his due, though, he usually sends his grandchildren a card and present at Christmas even though he rarely sees them."

"But you still keep in touch with your mother?" Matthews asked.

"Yes, we meet up at various times. She's the headmistress at the school here where Stella has recently joined the reception class, so I guess we'll be seeing her more frequently."

"Did you ever see Mike Brooks after he retired?"

"Yes." Leah gave a wry smile, and paused.

"Well?"

"We had a short fling while I was a student at Exeter University." She paused again then continued, "He's probably the father of my daughter, Lucy."

"Probably?"

"I'm not sure. I was a bit wild in those days."

"But the young girl, Stella ...."

"She's our daughter – I mean, by my partner, Chris. We've been together several years now. I've settled down to a respectable life, though we're not actually married. Yet."

Matthews thought she certainly gave the

impression of a young mother comfortable with her present situation. "Does Mike know about Lucy?"

"I've never told him. I haven't seen Mike for years, at least not to speak to. I'm not sure he'd even recognise me now."

Rachel doubted that, unless Leah had been really way out in her appearance in keeping with her declared wild nature. "Does Chris know about Mike?"

"No. He knows I had a child by a former lover but accepts that I don't know who the father was. He's been very good with her, and accepts her like his own daughter. Lucy's okay with him too. I suppose I've been very lucky to have found Chris."

"You've kept your own surname though."

"Yes, as I said, we're not married. Stella has a double-barrelled surname – she's Stella Burgess-Morgan. She quite enjoys being the only such one in her reception class."

"May I ask whether you are a working mother? Just for background really," said Rachel Allen. "It's not really relevant to our enquiries."

"I'm the manager of a florist's shop here in Budleigh, though the owner still does the odd couple of afternoons a week. Lucy also helps me out from time to time." Rachel's last comment then jogged Leah's memory, "Excuse me, what did you say you were investigating involving Mike Brooks?"

"A suspicious death. A supposed hit and run."

"Who was the victim?"

"His name was Robert Paisley."

Leah's cheeks went pale and her hands went to her mouth as she let out a cry.

Matthews was surprised by the unexpected reaction. "You knew him?"

"He's my cousin."

Des Matthews and Rachel Allen looked at each other given this revelation, all kinds of thoughts running through their minds at what new lines of enquiry this might open up. Many possible questions entered his head but he opted for a simple one." When did you last see Robert?"

"Not for a few days."

"Can you be more precise?"

"Er, it must have been two weeks ago, I suppose. Yes, Wednesday – it's my afternoon off."

"Do you see each other often?" Rachel Allen asked.

"No, quite rarely in normal circumstances."

"So what was abnormal about this occasion?" said Matthews.

Leah glanced anxiously out of the window before replying. "I'd asked him for help."

"With what?"

"My daughter Lucy was worried because she thought someone was following her – stalking her I mean. I asked Robert if he could look into it."

"Why didn't you report it to the police?"

"I wasn't sure there any real cause for concern, and without any real evidence I very much doubt that you would have done anything."

Matthew didn't let out that he was inclined to

agree. "When did this alleged stalking begin? "

"Probably about three weeks ago, but Lucy didn't tell me immediately."

"Did Robert find out anything?"

"Nothing definite when we last spoke, though he did say that he was working on another investigation."

"Did Lucy know that you had asked Robert to check on her concern?"

"Not precisely. I just thanked her for sharing her concern, and told her not to worry, I'd look into it. I passed on to Robert all the information that Lucy had given me."

"I see," Matthews said pensively. "May we talk to Lucy?"

"I'm expecting her soon," said Leah, again glancing out of the window. "She comes here quite often."

"She doesn't live with you then?" Rachel seemed quite surprised.

"She wanted some independence and when she was offered the small flat above the shop in return for a few hours working there we both thought it was a marvellous opportunity. I can keep a discreet eye on her."

"Sounds good," said Rachel.

"Okay, we'll leave it for now," said Matthews. "It would be useful to find out if she had had any glimpse of her stalker. He could be a possible suspect for the assault on Robert if he discovered his unnatural interest in Lucy might be exposed."

Matthews had completed a three point turn at the end of the cul-de-sec and had just passed Leah's house when Rachel noticed a young woman, probably in her late teens, come round the corner and walk towards them on the pavement. Pink roses on her white blouse matched the colour of her light skirt which exposed well-tanned and shapely legs several inches above her knees. She had long straight blonde hair down to her shoulders, and her spectacles, resting on a prominent nose, gave her a rather studious appearance.

"Sir, I wonder if that's Lucy."

Matthews pulled the car towards the kerb and parked on the single yellow line.

Rachel wound down the window and called out as the woman drew level, "Excuse me, are you Lucy Morgan?"

The young woman stopped and turned towards the car. "I'm sorry?"

Rachel repeated her question, and added "If so, we've just been speaking to your mother and we'd like a quick word with you as well, if that's okay." Rachel showed her warrant card and continued, "I'm D.S. Rachel Allen, and my boss here is D.I. Matthews.

"Yes, I'm Lucy," she said as she bent down to examine the card.

"Would you prefer to go to home or are you happy to talk here in the back of the car?" said Rachel. "It won't take long."

Lucy shrugged, "I'm okay here, I guess."

Rachel got out and opened the rear passenger door for Lucy, who climbed in.

"Lucy," Matthews began, "Your mother tells us that you have concerns about being stalked. Can you tell us more?"

"Not really. Just this feeling I had, like footsteps behind me. And I think I caught a glimpse of someone dodging into a doorway when I turned around. On more than one occasion I've seen the same person – a young man I think – in a hoodie standing across the road from the shop."

"That would be the florist's that your mother manages?"

"Yes, that's right." She paused for a moment then added, "I'm not sure whether it was the same person, but a few weeks back there was a young chap wearing a hoodie who came into the shop to buy flowers for his mother, so he said. Mum was out in the back of the shop and I was serving on my own."

"Can you describe him?"

"Not very well. Taller than me, quite slim, and I think he had fair hair beneath the hood. He was very polite and pleasant."

An idea entered Rachel's mind "Can you recall whether your sightings of this hooded man occurred at any at particular time or day?"

"Oh Christ, let me think about that..."

The detectives waited patiently.

After a couple of minutes Lucy replied, "The

purchase of flowers was definitely a Saturday. I can't be sure but I think the times when I saw him watching was afternoon – probably getting on towards closing time – and possibly a Saturday as well. And once in the evening, I think."

"Were you working late then?""

"No, I've got a flat above the shop. The owner used to live there until she retired."

"Well, thanks for talking to us, Lucy." Matthews handed her one of his cards. "If you think of anything else or if you think you see this fellow again please let us know. We'll let you get on home now. Oh, by the way," Matthews added as an afterthought, "Are you the learner driver for the Suzuki?"

"Yes, Mum's giving me lessons."

"Take care, now."

CHAPTER 11

"Paisley's flaming laptop"! About as much use as a water pistol in a a gun fight. Look at this!" Matthews handed a document from the sheaf on his desk to Rachel. "Seems to have wiped clean of any useful files, though they are trying to see if anything can be recovered from the hard drive."

"Nothing at all, sir?"

"Well, a long list of names in alphabetical order. Names of folders apparent, but absolutely nothing else, no other detail."

"What about fingerprints on the laptop?" Rachel asked.

"Paisley's obviously, and another set as yet unidentified."

"I'd guess that Paisley would have made a back up of all his files – but perhaps whoever broke in found that as well."

"Sod's law, you're probably right," Matthews grunted as took the next sheet and scanned it. "No ... yes!" His voice perked up, "Among the things forensics discovered at the flat was a pen drive stuffed under the mattress of his bed next to the wall!"

"That is good news, sir."

"Yes! Now, Rachel, please go downstairs and collect it. Bring it up and we'll see what we've got!"

A few minutes later, Rachel returned holding a small plastic coin bag containing a red SanDisc USB stick. "Interesting, sir, one would have expected to have found Paisley's prints on this."

"Whose were found then?"

"None whatsoever. No finger prints at all."

Matthews frowned, "Now that is distinctly odd. I assume that the pen drive was found in this bag – it's not something that forensics would have used. "

"That's correct, sir. And any prints on the bag were too smudged to be of any use."

"What about on the bed frame near where it was found?"

"I don't think they tested there."

Matthews picked up the phone, "Well, they are darn well going to do so now! No way would Paisley have bothered to clean it, and even if he had, his prints should be on that bed frame." He connected the USB stick to his laptop. "Let's see what we've got."

Rachel walked over to view the laptop screen. Opening up the USB device first displayed a long list of folders requiring a scroll down to view them all. By each folder a single name was displayed, occasionally followed by another letter. The folders, unsurprisingly, were in alphabetical order. "Seems he was kept pretty busy," she said.

"This is going to take one hell of a time to check through to see which, if any, are relevant to our enquiries." said Matthews.

Rachel grimaced. She had a pretty good idea whose time was going to be spent checking.

Matthews clicked at random a file named 'Hedges'. It opened to reveal a page headed 'Hedges, Maria – extra-marital affair, with contact address, email and telephone numbers. Below were several more folders named with dates, all from four years previously, and finally another folder labelled 'summary'. Opening that folder yielded about three-quarters of a page of text, which Matthews didn't bother reading in detail when he noticed the concluding statement: 'No action – case closed.'

He then opened another, named 'Roseberry' which again displayed the name followed by 'foreign workers' and a couple of dated folders.

"See what I mean?" Matthews brushed back his hair, frustrated.

Rachel looked more closely. "That one still seems to be on-going," she said, "the dates are all recent, and there's no summary."

"Try that landline number," said Matthews, pointing at the screen.

After a few rings, a woman's voice said, "Hello?"

"Is that Miss Roseberry?" asked Rachel

"It's Mrs, Mrs Miriam Roseberry. Who wants to know?" came the curt reply.

"This is Detective Sergeant Allen. We found you name and number on computer file belonging to a Robert Paisley." How did you know him?"

"Did?"

"I'm afraid he died in suspicious circumstances, which we are investigating."

"I'm sorry to hear that. When did he die?"

"Last Saturday. We think he may have been carrying out an investigation for you. Is that correct?"

"Yes, that's right. I wondered why I hadn't had any report back from him."

"What was the nature of his investigation? We just have the word 'foreign workers' against your name."

"Yes, lots of them and I very much doubt if they are registered. Working on a new development. I asked him to look into it."

"Why not the police?"

"I did, initially, but you lot didn't seem interested."

"I'm sorry about that," said Rachel, "Er, where exactly is this development? "

"In Topsham. Across the road from where I live."

"Had Robert made any reports back to you?"

"Not really, he hadn't been working on it very long. He told me he was going to speak to someone from the construction company. I suppose that's not going to happen now."

"I think we can say with confidence that, in connection with his death, we will be looking at that building site."

"Interesting," said Matthews as Rachel put the phone down, "But before we concentrate on Mrs Roseberry, check first to see if any other files give cause for concern."

Rachel scanned down the list of names assigned to the various folders. When she got to the bottom she asked her boss for the printed list he'd received from the computer geeks. "Sir, on this list there's the name Morgan but it's not on the USB stick list. Though all the other names are."

"You're right!" Matthews thumped the desk in frustration. "Why isn't there more information?"

"Perhaps it's because it's so recent that he hadn't got round to writing it up."

"That's as maybe but nothing? Not even the contact details or reason for investigation? Strikes me as very odd. We already know more about Paisley's investigation for Leah Morgan than that recorded digitally."

Matthews slumped back in his chair, deep in contemplation..

After a couple of minutes Rachel broke the silence. "Sir, may I share some thoughts with you?"

"Go ahead."

"I've been thinking about Brooks' statement. He claimed Paisley had spoken about Celia. But what if Paisley had actually said, 'see Leah'? It would make sense since he was both related to her and working for her. Brooks wouldn't have known about Paisley's connection to Celia or to Leah. Perhaps even Brooks killed Paisley."

"Why would he?"

"Perhaps he found out Paisley's connection to Leah and was worried his relationship might be exposed..."

"Why would that matter?" Matthews interjected.

Rachel was on a roll. "... Paisley goes to Brooks' home. They argue. Brooks strikes him down, drags him to Paisley's estate car, puts his own bike in the back, drives to the lane, dumps him in the field, then on to Woodbury Castle. Gets his bike out, sets fire to the car, pedals back to the field and pretends to discover the body."

Matthews didn't ridicule her theory but put some pertinent questions. "You've got a good imagination, Rachel, but why not leave the body in the car? Would he have had petrol handy to douse the vehicle? And why then go back to the field and even bother to mention Leah or Celia?"

"To divert suspicion?"

"Hmm. There is food for thought, and although it seems unlikely, stranger things have happened." Matthews considered for a moment then added, "Rachel, just to see if your suggestion does have any credibility, find out how long it would take to drive to Woodbury Castle from where Paisley was found, and how long to cycle back. Follow up any enquiries about cyclists along those roads early in the morning. We need to talk to Brooks again about some points, particularly his relationship with Leah."

CHAPTER 12

In the days following his unfortunate discovery Mike had taken other routes avoiding East Budleigh for his daily early morning exercise. He was beginning to realise however that the likelihood of history repeating itself was negligible, and he was also curious to see if another trip along the same lane might trigger memories hitherto buried in his mind.

His day didn't start well. He discovered the front tyre on his bicycle was flat, By the time he'd removed the small nail from the tyre, patched the inner tube and put everything back together again, it was after 7 am – more than an hour later than he normally set off. Inevitably then the roads were already getting busier. Today he had to wait for several vehicles to pass in each direction before he could cross the main B road from Newton Poppleford to Budleigh Salterton, and on narrow lanes more than once he had to pull over to let a car pass, even though he could have been selfish and make the vehicle crawl behind him. In East Budleigh village several people were giving their pet dogs their morning exercise. He turned into Hayes Lane and pedalled slowly. Glancing at the public car park he thought he recognised one of the parked cars. He stopped and looked but the number plate was indistinct with a smearing of mud, inevitably acquired on Devon's country lanes, and cream coloured Ford Fiestas were pretty common anyway. He continued along the lane, past a few thatched cottages, and turned as he had done before into the lane leading towards Yettington. Avoiding a large pothole, he dismounted when he came to the gateway where he had found Paisley. He was not really expecting to find anything that the police had missed, and, apart from an increase in the number of footprints in the entrance, nothing looked any different. The police tape had been removed. He could see the boulder, still with a dark stain on it, where Paisley must have hit his head but it was a few feet away from where he had lain. Had he crawled or even staggered a short distance, Mike wondered. His curiosity satisfied, Mike continued on his journey, partly on foot where the lane became steeper. He knew that he last part of his journey would be much less tiring, being mainly downhill.

As he approached his house, the general feeling of contentment that had eventually come through his ride disappeared when he saw a car that he definitely recognised draw up. He couldn't think why on Earth the police would want to speak to him again.

"Good morning, Mr Brooks," said Matthews, "Just finished your morning exercise?"

"Uh huh," Mike replied, resignedly, "You'd best come inside." He wheeled his bike up the drive and propped it against the wall. "I'm going to get a cup of coffee before I talk to you again. Do you want one? You're up and about your business early today."

"We're okay, thanks," Matthews replied, and resisted airing the comment that came to mind about the early bird catching the worm. He didn't think it would get them off to a good start. Not that Brooks would be particularly happy anyway with their questions today.

"So what's it all about this time," said Mike a few minutes later when he had settled himself down with a large steaming mug of freshly brewed coffee. "I thought I had answered all your questions."

"You have answered our questions but there are one or two points that we need to revisit. Firstly, though, did you see an estate car or did one pass you when you were cycling?"

"Definitely not."

"I'd like you to think back very carefully to what you heard Paisley say before he died. You mentioned 'Tell Celia' but is that strictly correct? Did you in fact hear anything?"

Mike frowned, "Why would I make it up?"

"You tell me."

"I'm not sure where you are going with this questioning. Are you suggesting I lied?"

Matthews ignored his question. "Okay, so what precisely did he say? Please think carefully."

Mike paused, forehead furrowed. "It sounded like 'Celia tell her'"

"Not 'tell Celia'?"

"No, I'm sure I'm right now."

"We know Paisley's ex-girlfriend was called Celia but could he have said 'See Leah – tell her'?"

Mike looked at Matthews in astonishment "But why would he want to tell Leah?"

"Tell her who had attacked him, perhaps?"

"But we – you, I mean, – don't know who attacked him."

"Did you know Leah and Robert were cousins?"

Again Mike showed surprise. "No, no idea at all."

"Not from school?"

"They were not there at the same time."

"As well as being related, Leah had also asked him to investigate someone whom Lucy thought might be stalking her." Matthews added, "That's Leah's daughter – and your daughter too probably, so Leah told us"

"What!" Mike's eyes almost shot through the roof of his head.

"You haven't been entirely honest with us, Mr Brooks. You told us that you had not been in touch with Leah since she left school, but that isn't true, is it? You had a relationship with her when she was at university."

Mike looked dejected. "That was just a one night stand. She has never told me that we had a daughter."

"It wasn't you stalking Lucy?"

"No, of course not! Why would I if I didn't know about her?"

"One last thing, do you drive a car?"

"Yes, I've got a small Nissan Micra. Don't use it very much, mostly for the odd shopping trip or to the theatre in Exeter.

"Is there anything else that might be relevant to our enquiries that you haven't yet told us?" said Matthews.

Mike held his head in his hands. The revelation that he probably had a daughter whom he had never met and probably would have never known about had it not been for Paisley's demise generated many different competing emotions in his mind. "No I don't think so," he eventually answered almost in a whisper.

"You are sure you had not met Robert Paisley at any time since he left school?"

"Of that I am certain. I have had no contact with him whatsoever."

"Very well," Matthews closed his notebook and switched off the voice recorder on his phone, happy that Brooks had at the outset agreed to the conversations being recorded. "We will leave you to finish your breakfast. You know how to contact us – although I understand that your son is a constable based in Exmouth with us."

"Yes, that's right. He took a post-graduate teacher training course but then decided he didn't want to follow in my footsteps".

After they had departed, Mike brewed another coffee and ate the croissant he'd bought at the village shop on the way home. Flopping then into an armchair he closed his eyes and tried to bring some order to the various thoughts that were filling his head arising from the recent interview.

He smiled as his mind wandered back to the occasion when he had last met Leah. It was a year that Exeter was hosting the annual Inter-Varsity Folk Dance Festival. He had been keen on folk dancing when he was at Exeter University and had taken part in a couple of the festivals at other venues up country. Though his interest had waned somewhat in recent years, he and Freda had enjoyed going to a ceilidh from time to time and had even been members of a folk dance club in Exmouth for a couple of years. The weekend of the IVFDF event in Exeter Freda was visiting her parents in Southampton and had taken their young son, Steven with her. Simon was also away on a school trip. With nothing particular to keep him at home Mike had decided to go to the Saturday evening ceilidh. He'd caught sight of Leah first. In a low-cut party dress she had looked even more attractive than as a sixth former in school uniform. When she had spotted him she had left the small group of girls with whom she had been chatting and had immediately come over to this table "Mr Brooks," she had said, "What a lovely surprise to see you here," He'd responded in a similar manner and invited her to call him Mike since they were no longer student and teacher. Leah had forsaken her friends and had spent the rest of the evening with him, leading him on to the floor as a willing partner into ceilidh dances, to the excellent rhythmic music of the Bismarcks Band. As the evening had drawn to a close, happy in her company and feeling carefree from the effect of several drinks during the evening, he had offered to walk her home. He had left his car in the car park, knowing that it wouldn't have been wise to drive anyway. Knowing that she had lived not that far away while still at school, he had been quite surprised that she had opted for student accommodation rather than living at home. Leah's student pad was no more than ten minutes walk from the student's union building and he had accepted her invite to come in for a nightcap. Next morning they had parted, each without regrets at the night they had spent in each other's arms and neither wishing to make it an on-going relationship.

Mike didn't know whether to feel happy or sad that Leah had never contacted him when she had found herself pregnant nor told him about her daughter Lucy. He realised that he was very fortunate that Leah's silence had meant he'd not had to face a difficult situation with Freda about his one night of infidelity, nor that that he'd fathered a daughter out of wedlock.

When he'd had to face resigning his long-held teaching post he had at first been very resentful of Leah for putting him into a vulnerable position and he had also been angered by her father's desire to pursue the matter even though both he and Leah knew there was no justification. In retrospect, however, he had enjoyed the freedom that early retirement had brought him.

CHAPTER 13

Leah faced a dilemma. Now that she had mentioned to the police that Mike Brooks was probably the father of Lucy, that information which she had always withheld from both Mike and Lucy, and also her partner, Chris, was bound to come to their attention. Almost certainly it had done so already with Mike if the police had spoken to him again. She decided it would be far better to tell Lucy herself rather than let her hear from gossip or on social media. But unless both Lucy and Mike agreed to have a DNA test, her father would still be a matter of speculation. It would also mean that she would have to get in touch with Mike and she could not be sure what his reaction would be after having been kept in the dark all these years.

Leah considered she had been fortunate. She had been able to complete her business studies degree before her pregnancy became too advanced. Her mother had given her unreserved support, and, as headmistress of a primary school, had arranged for her to take up a secretarial post there, and have the baby with her. Her father, however, if he had still been married to her mother, would have dismissed her as being an irresponsible tart, and banned her from ever setting foot in the family home again, in which case she may have had to consider approaching Mike for some support for the child.

She glanced at the clock. Lucy would be arriving soon for another driving lesson in her mother's Suzuki.

In the daylight of the early summer evenings the roads were usually fairly quite after any commuters had returned home from work. Leah took Lucy on their usual circular route down to Budleigh Salterton seafront then up the B road to Newton Poppleford before heading towards Exeter and back via Woodbury. Until Lucy became more confident and proficient, particularly in reversing, Leah avoided taking her along any of the many narrow country roads in their area.

Lucy completed a successful three point turn in the cul-de-sac to park outside her mother's house in the right direction for the next time the car was used.

"Have you got a while before you head back to your flat," Leah said, "I've got something I'd like to talk to you about."

"No worries," said Lucy, "Nothing else planned for this evening."

A cup of coffee in their hands they both took to an

armchair. Leah still felt rather uneasy about raising the issue. "You know already, Lucy, that you were born quite a long time before I met Chris, though he accepts you practically as his own daughter."

Lucy nodded, wondering where her mother was going with this.

"I've never been certain beyond all doubt about the identity of your father, but I am pretty sure I know who he is."

Lucy face took a serious look, "Go on."

"One consequence of the interview by the police the other day is that he is also now aware that he has a teenage daughter. The only way we can be certain is if you both agreed to have a DNA test. Would you be willing?"

Lucy considered the question, her forehead creased in thought. "I suppose so," she eventually replied, then smiled, "It would be good to know where I came from."

Leah breathed a sigh of relief that her daughter had taken the matter calmly — and sensibly. "Would you like to meet him?"

"Yes, certainly, if he is indeed my father." She then added, "Who are we talking about?"

"I think it would be better to get confirmation before you know his name, just in case I'm been mistaken."

Lucy nodded.

"I haven't spoken to him yet. Haven't spoken to him for about eighteen years, in fact, but I know he lives in this area, and, now with your consent, I will try and arrange a meeting. Just the two of us initially, and then if he is agreeable, we can all meet."

"I'm okay with that."

As they stood up and Lucy prepared to leave, Leah held her in a hug. "Thank you for being so understanding. You're precious to me."

"You're a big softee, Mum." Another hug.

When Lucy had left, Leah now considered the problem of how she was going to get in touch with Mike. She knew he lived somewhere in the area but had no clue where. He might know where she had lived as a schoolgirl and he had spent a night at her student pad but he'd never mentioned his address at any time. A telephone directory might help, if he had a land line registered with BT and he would be on the electoral roll but that would require a lot of time, even if she knew where to focus her search.

A possible solution came as she was lying in bed next morning, waiting for her partner to vacate the bathroom. It was too early for her to act immediately but as soon as she got to work and before she opened up the shop for customers, she rang the police station and asked to speak to Inspector Matthews.

"It's Leah Morgan here," she said when he'd answered the phone, "I would like to meet with Mike Brooks, since you are likely to have mentioned that he is probably Lucy's father. Can you let me have either his address or phone number?"

Matthews thought carefully before replying. "I can confirm that we did mention the possibility when we last interviewed him. I don't think we could release his contact details without his permission."

"Can you ask him, please?"

"I can do that for you. Would you like me to ask him to give you a call?"

"Er, no. I think I'd rather make the decision when to speak to him. If he's agreeable to me contacting him, just let me have the details."

"Very well. Oh by the way, while you are on the phone, we have recovered a USB stick belonging to Robert Paisley, with information about his various investigations. We've still got to work through that data but we noticed that among the named folders was 'Morgan' but absolutely nothing else when we opened it. You did say that you had asked him to look at a possible stalking of Lucy."

"Yes, that's correct."

"Did he give any indication at all about whether he'd found out anything. I believe we did ask you that question earlier but something may have come to mind."

"No, I'm sorry. He said he had a suspicion but needed to do some more checks."

CHAPTER 14

Rachel Allen tapped on the door of her inspector's office.

"Good morning, Rachel, you look as if you've got something to tell me," said Matthews.

"Good morning sir. Not sure how useful it will be. To get by car to Woodbury Castle from where the body was found would take five minutes at best, ten minutes at the most. It's barely three miles away."

"Okay. And getting back by bike?"

"A lot of it is downhill, so fifteen minutes at the outside I'd say."

"So if your theory was correct, Brooks would have been back with Paisley within about half an hour?"

"That would be pushing it given that he'd have to get his bike out of the vehicle and set the car on fire."

"Hmm, I think we are realistically looking at another culprit."

"I've also been through Paisley's files on the memory stick. Most we can put to one side as they are at least two years old or are minor affairs that wouldn't warrant killing the investigator. So I think, sir, we should look more closely at the Roseberry file."

"Okay, no time like the present. Let's see what he was up to."

The first entry was dated four weeks ago.

Visited Miriam Roseberry. Retired widow. Still owns florist shop in Budleigh.

Concerned about foreign workers on building site opposite house. Initial fee agreed.

No obvious cause for concern from view from window.

There then followed a series of reports on each of the following three days.

7am Minibus arrived. Sixteen men. Half ethnic Indian or Arab. Two black. Others white probably Mediterranean. Some conversation – not English. Site gates opened by white male from small portacabin. Office? Foreman? Some JCBs still on site. House construction already started. Vehicle check – registered to SiEmsCo.

6 pm Minibus returns & loaded. Followed to isolated farm south of Honiton.

7am Minibus arrived. Same men.

Followed empty minibus but lost at by M5 junction.

Visited farm – looks abandoned. Minibus just parked there. Driver goes to farmhouse. Observed site for possible access. Delivery of bricks & timber.

6.00 am Farm Gained access after minibus left.

Kitchen in use. Porridge remains. Basic bathroom. No rooms upstairs used – leaky roof.

Bunk bed downstairs – both used. Old stable block padlocked. Gained access. Sleeping bags on straw in most bays. Long wooden table & wooden benches. Cold water sink. Several dirty latrine buckets.

3 pm On site. Council surveyor. Foreign workers labouring. Brief chat to one – Iraqi Few words of English. Site manager stopped any further talk. Asked for my name as I left, Burgess.

The next entries were a week later

Late delivery. Gates opened. Workers gathering for minibus. Asian man broke free and ran out of gate. Chased and grabbed. Intervened. Worker had livid gash on right cheek. Ran off. His captor smaller than me – gave up trying to fight. Gates closed with workers inside. Minibus went after escapee. Followed minibus. No sighting.

Check on company name SiEmsCo. Registered Office Exeter. Directors Clive Mitchell, <u>Charles Morgan.</u> Leah's father? Tell her?

Nothing further appeared.

"Well, it certainly looks as if he was on to something with that company," said Matthews.

"Strange name for a business though," Rachel commented.

"Not really. Look at the directors' names. Both have the initials C and M. SiEms, see?"

"Oh bloody hell – er, sorry, sir – obvious!"

"And did Paisley tell her – tell Leah?" said

Matthews. "Something we'll need to ask her again. But there is something else here that caught my eye," he continued. "Remember I mentioned I'd been called to view a body washed up on a beach?"

Rachel nodded.

"Well, I recall there was a large wound on the right cheek of the victim. Could be the same person that Paisley saw."

"Shame we can't ask him, "said Rachel.

"Indeed, but we can see if any of the other workers are able to identify him. I'll need to get some photos from the mortuary. With our investigation on-going, they won't have buried or cremated him yet."

"Why do you think he gave the name 'Burgess'?

Matthews shrugged. "First thing that came to mind? But check with the Council to see they actually have anyone with that name employed as a surveyor. In the meantime, we'll find out what Mr Charles Morgan has to say for himself." Another thought came to his mind. "By the way, talking of Morgan, did you find any more on the pen drive for the Morgan file that appeared on the laptop?"

"No sir. Not even a folder named Morgan."

When his sergeant had left to contact the Council, Matthews rang Leah's mobile, as he expected that she would still be at work.

She answered after several rings and when the caller identified himself she promised to call him back in a few minutes as she had a customer with her. "Okay, Leah here, Inspector Matthews. Is this about contacting Mike?"

"Thanks for reminding me. If you've got a pen, here's his details. He is willing for you to get in touch." Matthews waited a moment before giving the information. "But that wasn't the reason for my call. We have recovered a USB stick with details of your cousin's investigation, and there a couple of points that I need to ask about."

"Okay."

"Firstly, did Robert ever mention to you that one of his investigations had led him to suspect that your father might be involved in some, er, dodgy activities?"

"What? No, he never said anything to me – though I wouldn't put it past my father to get involved in anything – I presume you mean illegal – if he thought he could make money and get away with it."

"On the USB stick there was a comment, 'Tell Leah?' as if he was undecided. It might have been the reason for what Mike Brooks thought he said.

"I'm not quite sure what he would have wanted me to do with any information. As I have already told you, I have as little to do with my father as possible, and I know the feeling is mutual. Where incidentally, is this building site?"

"In Topsham. It's a new development opposite a house which is the home of the person who engaged Robert because of her concerns. She apparently retired there for peace and quiet."

"Oh? Just wonder if that might have been the owner of this shop, Rosie's, She retired to Topsham."

"What is her name?

"Roseberry, Miriam Roseberry."

"That is her." Matthews didn't like the fact that there was yet another apparently coincidental link to his enquiries but couldn't see any obvious connection to pursue at this point in time. "Robert also appears to have pretended to be a Council surveyor to gain access to the building site that your father's company was working on, and he gave the name 'Burgess' when challenged."

"Oh the stupid bastard!" Leah exclaimed, "How could he!"

"Pardon?" said Matthews, even more surprised by her reaction.

"Chris Burgess is my partner. And he works for the Council as a surveyor."

"Do you think he would have told Chris?"

"God knows! Christ, to think I even trusted him to find out if anyone was stalking Lucy!"

"That's actually the next point. Although there was a folder labelled 'Morgan' on his laptop there is absolutely nothing on the memory stick, Not even an empty Morgan folder. Are you sure he didn't say anything about whom he suspected?"

"Nothing. Nothing at all. Look I have to go now, another customer has just come in."

"That's okay." Matthews exhaled as he put the phone down. "For the time being."

Inevitably he would now have to speak with Leah's partner to see if Paisley had imparted any information to him.

CHAPTER 15

Mike was already seated at a table sipping a coffee when he saw Leah enter. Though he hadn't seen her for over seventeen years, he recognised her immediately. She had the shapely slim figure he remembered and, though slightly fuller in the face, her skin was still smooth and wrinkle free. Only her blonde hair was shorter, neatly cut just above her shoulders rather than half way down her back. Though the cafe was fairly busy, she quickly caught sight of him and walked over. Mike stood to greet her. "Leah! I'm so pleased to see you! Can I get you a coffee or tea?"

"Coffee would be fine, An Americano with hot milk."

She took the spare seat at the table. "Thank you so much for agreeing to meet me," she said when Mike returned with her drink, "It's been a long time."

"It's my pleasure. The years have been kind to you. You're still a very attractive woman." Mike realised that might sound too forward. "Sorry, that was not meant to be a chat up line."

Leah smiled. "I think we've both moved on from that." She paused, considering carefully how to address the main reason for their meeting. "It's unlikely that we would be sitting here talking had it not been for the police investigation into the death of Robert Paisley. Did you know he was my cousin?"

Mike shook his head. "No, I didn't. I'm really sorry."

"We weren't close," Leah took a deep breath. "Anyhow, I think you now know that you are probably the father of Lucy, my daughter."

"Yes, the police did mention it. Why did you never tell me?"

"I couldn't be sure. I didn't want to put a threat to your marriage and possibly cause your children to cope with their parents separating. I had good support from my mother in raising Lucy, and I'm now in a long and steady relationship with my partner. We have a daughter of our own – she's now five years old – and Chris treats Lucy as he would his own child, even though he knows he is not the father."

"Does he know that I am?"

"No. As I said, I'm not certain. Although I can see you in Lucy's features."

"What about Lucy? How much does she know?"

"She has always known that Chris is not her biological father but they get on very well together. We've both been very lucky. As I feared the issue would probably come into the open as a result of the police enquiries I have talked with Lucy and asked her if she would be willing to take a DNA test to resolve the question once and for all."

"Has she agreed?"

"If you also agree to be tested. I haven't yet told Chris about this but intend to do so if results confirm you are Lucy's father.

"Will it be a problem if he knows?"

"No I don't think so. I don't think he would see you as any threat."

"I won't be."

"Does that mean you'll agree to the DNA test?"

"Yes. I think it would be good for Lucy to know. And I'd be delighted to know that I've got a teenage daughter as well as two sons." Mike paused before adding, "If I am her dad, that is, I'd really like to meet her. If she's agreeable."

"Can we meet up again? When we know the result?"

"I'd like that."

Lucy stood up, "Till then."

Mike followed her outside. "Thank you, Leah." he said, taking her hand. "May I?"

Leah nodded. He raised her hand to his lips and kissed it.

CHAPTER 16

Matthews looked at the photographs which Rachel Allen handed him. Though various sea creatures and probably gulls had fed on the corpse's face, leaving empty eye sockets and damage around the mouth and nose, the large scar across the victim's right cheek was clearly evident, as were the brownish colour to the skin and the ethnic features of a person from the Indian sub-continent. "How long had he been in the water?"

"Rough estimate from the pathologist is three or four days, sir," Rachel replied. "Interesting thing is, no sea water in his lungs."

"So he was dead before he entered the water?"

"Apparently so."

"I wonder why we've not had any notification about this already."

"I think the post mortem's only just been carried out. No urgency flagged up and nobody of his description reported missing."

"Hmm. Looks as if we've got another unexplained death on our hands. And another reason to talk to Charles Morgan." Matthews stroked in chin, "Rachel, I want you to take these photos and go over to the building site in Topsham. See if you can get anybody there to identify this bloke." He gestured with his thumb towards a six-foot tall, broad-shouldered young man in the office. "Better take young D.C. Watkins with you as backup just in case you get any aggro. I don't think anyone would want to mess with him."

Rachel made to leave when Matthews spoke again. "Also while you're there have a word with Mrs Roseberry. It's just possible she might recognise him."

Matthews made himself a coffee from the machine he'd bought for his office and sat back in his chair to go over in his mind what the investigation had revealed so far. There seemed to be many threads, loose ends that he hoped he would be able to connect. There was something that was niggling him – a chance remark or a titbit of information that seemed insignificant at the time, but could prove crucial – if he could only remember what it was. Another thought came to him, and he checked for a phone number on his laptop.

"Good morning, is Christopher Burgess available?"

"Yes, I think so," replied the receptionist at the Council Offices, "Who shall I say is calling?"

"It's Detective Inspector Matthews. It's nothing to worry about. He may be able to help me on a particular query."

"Okay, I'll put you through."

The call tone was answered after a couple of rings.

"Good morning, Inspector, how can I help you?"

"Thank you, Mr Burgess. I'm sure you are aware that we are investigating the death of Robert Paisley "

"Yes, Leah has mentioned it."

"Did she mention that Paisley has used your identity to gain access to a building site in Topsham?"

"Yes. Silly man."

"Now, I'm wondering whether he just used your identity because he knew about your job from his cousin, or whether he had been in touch with you directly."

"As a matter of fact he did contact me."

"When was this?"

"Let me see, two or three weeks ago, I think. I can check in my diary."

"That's probably not necessary. Can you tell me the purpose of his call?"

"Basically, whether I had heard any rumours or seen anything to raise my suspicion about illegal immigrant workers on site?"

"And had you?"

"Not really. I have visited the site from time to time and there were some, shall we say, obviously not ethnic white there, but that is not unusual in itself."

"I presume that you are also aware that the construction company is owned by Leah's father.

Does that present any conflict of interest if you suspected that Charles Morgan might be doing anything illegal?"

Chris Burgess chuckled. "You must be joking. Leah hates her father, and will have nothing to do with him."

"I understand," said Matthews. "Thanks for talking to me."

As the conversation concluded and raised no new concerns, Matthews had an instant flash of awareness of the issue that had niggled him. "The USB stick!" he muttered to himself. Why was there absolutely no record on it of Paisley's investigation into Lucy's stalking whereas his laptop had a folder labelled Morgan? And why clear of any fingerprints? He realised he hadn't yet received a report on whether any prints other than Paisley's had been found on the bed frame where the device had been found.

* * *

Rachel Allen returned soon after lunch to report back what she had found. "No joy with identifying the body from the sea, although I think the site foreman was lying. He denied ever seeing the bloke but his eyes suggested otherwise when I showed him the photo."

"What about other workers on the site?" Matthews asked.

"That's the strange thing, sir. Not one dark-skinned worker there, as far as either of us could see. And no-one could – or would – recognise the poor chap from the photo."

"Did you have any problem gaining access?"

"Not really. Chap on the gate was uncooperative and demanded to see a warrant. Which I said we could easily get but as we only wanted to show a photograph I suggested it would be far less hassle to let us in. Which he did, reluctantly."

"Any better luck with Mrs Roseberry ?"

Rachel shook her head. "She said it could have been one of the foreigners but she was too far away to make a positive identification. Also, she mentioned that the minibus with them hasn't been there for the last few days."

"Hmm. Seems as if the boss is covering his tracks." Matthews thought for a moment. "Right, next thing, we're going to find the farm that Paisley mentioned – and get a forensics team ready to do fingerprints and DNA search. We may get lucky and find some evidence of clothing to match the foreign body. Remind me, where did Paisley say it was?"

"Um, not very precise, sir. Isolated, south of Honiton."

Matthews loaded Google Maps onto his laptop and centred on the area of interest. "Rachel, I want you to look in detail at the ariel view of the region bounded by the A35 Honiton to Axminster road, the A375 Honiton to Sidmouth, and the A3052 Sidford to Colyford. There's a whole spider's web of minor road. Start at the western edge and work towards Colyton. Use the roadway view as well and see if you can come up with some possibilities. It will be better than looking for a needle in a haystack!"

CHAPTER 17

"It's Leah. Would you like to meet me at the cafe again? Either lunchtime or after I've finished work, whichever suits you best."

"I'd be delighted," Mike replied, "Lunchtime would be fine. Have you got the results?"

"I'll tell you when we meet. Shall we say one o'clock?"

"Look forward to it."

It wasn't often that his work took him to Budleigh Salterton but there had been a planning application for an extension to a property near the sea front which the Council wanted him to look at. He expected his late morning appointment to last not much more than an hour and Chris thought it would be a pleasant surprise to pop into Rosie's and take Leah out for a pub lunch. As he drove slowly along the street, looking for a short term parking space, he saw Leah leave her florist's shop about a hundred yards ahead and start walking away from him along the pavement a short distance. Until she came to a cafe where she was greeted by a older gent who kissed her hand and led her into the cafe, with his arms round her shoulders.

His initial surprise gave way to mixed emotions and conjectures as to what she was up to. Chris managed to pull in just beyond the cafe, where he had a clear view of the door through his passenger side mirror. Thoughts of lunch abandoned, he felt compelled to wait and watch. His half-hour permitted parking expired, Chris remained where he was, hoping that no parking warden would turn up before Leah and her companion left the cafe. Some fifty minutes later, pushing his luck, Chris caught sight of a warden approaching on the other side of the road just as Leah reappeared. The man embraced her, kissed her, this time on the lips, and turned towards Chris as Leah hurried back to the shop. Chris rejected the impulse to get out of the car and confront the bloke, ask what the hell he was doing, and pulled out before the warden could reach him. Chris followed the man, who he could now see was almost certainly well into his sixties, into the car park where he unlocked a Nissan Micra and drove off. Chris was tempted to follow him but remembered he was due back at his office for an afternoon meeting.

Chris couldn't get the image of what he had witnessed out of his mind, and realised he had probably not seemed fully attentive to his colleagues' discussions during the meeting. He knew a little about Leah's past, knew that she had slept around as a teenager and during her college days, but he had been sure, until now, that any promiscuous activity was behind her and that she was a faithful partner to him – as he was to her. His feelings were more puzzlement and disappointment rather than anger but he knew he would have to face her and get the truth as to what was happening. Unable to concentrate on his work any longer he left the meeting as soon as his meeting had ended and made his way home

He didn't expect Leah back until four o'clock as she would be collecting their young daughter from school. An hour to consider how best to approach the delicate issue. He poured himself a large whisky and as he slumped in the armchair he noticed a light flashing on the telephone. He picked up the receiver and entered the code for saved messages.

"Lovely to see you again, Leah. You know I've always had a soft spot for you. Look forward to Saturday evening."

He looked at the diary beside the phone. For today there was an entry which read ' M. 1 pm'. Checking back he found another entry with M and a time. "Shit, shit, SHIT!" he swore.

Chris was still in the armchair when Leah arrived home. Stella ran over to him for the usual cuddle she expected from her father but stopped, bewildered, when he told her curtly to go to her room. She looked at Leah, and bolted from the room, crying.

"What on Earth's the matter with you, Chris?"

Leah snapped, in annoyance. She spied the half empty bottle of whisky on the table. "You've been drinking!"

"Yes, and you've been whoring! Back to your old ways!"

"What! What the hell are you talking about?"

"I saw you today in Budleigh. I was going to take you for lunch but your lover got their first."

"You're not making any sense, Chris. I haven't got another lover. No-one else but you."

Chris stood up and faced her, his voice rising in anger, "You deny it? You were hugging and kissing. And it's not the first time is it? And you've already got your weekend planned, haven't you!" He grabbed the phone and punched in the code. "Listen to this!"

Leah tentatively took the handset and listened. She put the phone down and turned to Chris, a defiant expression on her face. "That was Mike Brooks," she almost spat out the words, "I have just confirmed that he is Lucy's father …"

"And you're now renewing your affair!" Chris shouted.

Leah had never seen Chris lose his temper before. She tried to keep her voice calmer. "Not at all! We met at lunchtime so that I could tell him the result of the paternity test, and make arrangements for Lucy to meet him."

"She knows but you didn't tell me?"

"She knows now but I didn't want to tell you until I was sure."

"I don't believe you!" Chris headed for the front door, turning back to yell, "You can take Lucy with you to your Mike and I'll keep Stella!"

He slammed the door and she heard the car start. She rushed out just to see the car accelerate away. "Chris!" she called in vain, "For Christ's sake don't drive!"

She went back in and sat down with her head in her hands, despairing what to do.

"Mummy?" Stella tottered up to her.

"Poppet," said Leah, taking her in her arms.

"What is wrong with Daddy?"

"He ... he's had a bad day at work, my love," Leah tried to sooth her, "It'll be alright." She said, but with little confidence that the outcome would be that easy.

CHAPTER 18

"I think I've found the farmhouse, sir," Rachel greeted her boss the next morning. "Or at least I've narrowed it down to two possibilities." She picked up a local Ordnance Survey map to show Matthews. "This one seems to be the most likely," she said, pointing to a spot among a network of country lanes north of the Sidford to Seaton road and quite separated from the nearest village.

"Well done, Rachel. Right, we'll head over there now and have a look," said Matthews. "Alert the forensics team. And we'll also need backup in case there any troublesome characters on site. Oh, and make sure you have that map with you. We don't want to get lost chasing our tails."

Matthews and Allen in their unmarked vehicle followed the patrol car along the narrow muddy lanes. In the unlikely event of meeting any oncoming traffic the sight of a police car would surely stop any confrontation as to who should give way and back up.

"Certainly is off the beaten track," Matthews

commented to Rachel as they pulled into the yard of the farm which had been identified as the likely hideout of the foreign workers.

The site appeared deserted. No minibus was present, although tyre marks in the mud indicated that at least one vehicle had been there since the last rainfall a few days earlier. From the exterior, the decrepit farmhouse seemed to match the description in Paisley's notes, and once inside, through the unlocked front door, the downstairs bunk beds and kitchen obviously used recently, all added confirmation that they had found the correct location. Matthews made a call, agreeably surprised that there was a strong signal, to bring in the forensics, then headed across the yard with his colleague to a stable block, the doors of which were gently swinging in the south-westerly breeze. When they entered a nauseous stench assaulted their nostrils from a pile of human excrement that had spilled from an old metal bucket lying on its side. Holding their nose, they explored further. Some used cutlery and metal plates had been left on the table. No sleeping bags were seen in any of the stalls although the straw left there certainly looked as if it had had something – or someone – heavy on top of it.

"Sir, come and look at this!" Rachel had just entered the penultimate stall and called to her boss when she spotted the discolouration on a small patch of straw.

Matthews quickly joined her from the other

end of the row and bent down to examine the stall more closely. He also looked at the adjoining wooden partition. "I'd place a bet that we're looking at bloodstains. Human blood if we're lucky." He stood up and folded his arms. "This is going to take the team quite a while, he said thoughtfully, "I'll want this blood tested, all those plates and cutlery tested for fingerprints – and all the buckets of shit. "

"Going through the motions, sir?" said Rachel with a smile.

Matthews grinned too, "You're in the wrong profession, Rach, you should have been a stand-up comedian."

Rachel held her tongue. She thought saying 'comedienne' to correct his comment would be counterproductive to the touch of humour in a serious investigation.

"It would be good if they can also find some fibres off sleeping bags and items of clothing. And there's the farmhouse to be checked as well. I think Paisley made a note of the minibus registration, so if we put out a search notice for it we may be lucky and find where all these people have been relocated."

The two uniformed officers from the patrol car reported back that they had found no other signs of recent human activity elsewhere on the farm beyond the yard. Matthews thanked them and sent them back to their normal duties.

"You know, Rachel," Matthews mused as they

sat waiting in their car to brief the forensics team when they arrived, "looking around the countryside here you'd think we were in the middle of bugger all rather than a couple of miles from seaside resorts."

"That's probably why this old farm was chosen. Grockles from the cities aren't happy to get their precious new cars scratched by brambles and plastered in mud by venturing down these glorified farm tracks."

Matthews chuckled. "You're probably right. Ah!, here come the boys," he said as two white vans drove into the yard. "I'll have a word with them then we can be off to see what Charles Morgan has to say. It's on the way home."

* * *

The offices of SiEmsCo could easily have been missed by a casual passer-by. Just a small name plaque on the pillar adjoining the gate into the driveway of a large detached house in the Woolbrook area of Sidmouth was the only indication that the property was anything other than a substantial private dwelling. A discreet arrow in the grassy verge beside the footpath to the front door directed them to a single storey extension that bordered onto the driveway to a double garage. A shiny new BMW occupied one space.

Matthews tapped on the door to the extension

and then tried the handle, which opened into a small reception area. Behind the desk a sharp-featured woman with greying shoulder length hair and large spectacles looked up at them as they entered.

"Do you have an appointment?" she said rather brusquely.

"No, we ...."

"Then I'm afraid Mr Morgan is not available." the receptionist interrupted.

"I'm sure he will be," said Matthews, presenting his own warrant card, and introducing D.S. Allen, "We need to speak with him."

Initially taken aback by the presence of police officers, the receptionist quickly recovered. "May I ask what this about?"

"You may ask but the matter is strictly between us and Mr Morgan. May I ask your name?"

"I'm his wife, Kelly-Ann Morgan."

"Thank you, Mrs Morgan." said Matthews and gestured with his eyes towards the door leading, he supposed, to Morgan's inner sanctum.

She rose from her chair and they followed her into a small rear corridor with a toilet and small kitchen on one side. She tapped on the panelled wooden door at the end, and opened it. "These police officers would like a word with you, Charles," she said, stepping back to let them inside, before retreating back to her reception area.

The room was simply but purposely furnished with two four-drawer wooden filing cabinets, a bookshelf, cupboard, two padded chairs, and a large mahogany desk behind which sat Charles Morgan. Matthews would have put him in his late fifties or early sixties. He still had a full head of hair, greying but short and neatly combed back. His face was rugged and reddened around the cheeks, as if he had spent much of his life working outdoors in all weathers. His sharp blues eyes and the shape of his mouth were similar to those of Leah, although Matthews guessed she probably took more after her mother. Though obviously working from home, he was still smartly dressed, in a dark grey suit, white shirt and a tie which was probably from his old school or college. His suit jacket was draped over the back of his office chair.

He stood up to greet them and extended his arm for a handshake.

"Thank you for seeing us," Matthews began.

"I doubt if I really had any choice about that," Morgan replied. "Anyway, take a seat and tell me what this visit is all about."

"We are investigating the suspicious death of Robert Paisley, whose body was found near East Budleigh just over a week ago."

"Yes?" Morgan's face showed no recognition or emotion.

"Did you know him?"

"'Fraid not"

"What about your business partner, Clive Mitchell?"

Charles gave a throaty laugh, "Clive? He's long

dead and buried. It's been just me for the last few years."

"But the business is still registered to both of you."

"Is it? I must have forgotten to update the information." Morgan said dismissively.

"Obviously this is your admin centre but can you tell me where your, er, works depot is? Where you keep your machinery, vehicles and stock of building materials."

"We've got a yard at Exeter, on the Sowton Industrial Estate."

"Thank you. Now are you sure you didn't know Paisley? Your daughter, Leah, is his cousin."

"He must be from my wife's – my ex-wife's – side of the family."

"And you've never met?"

"I didn't have much to do with her relatives, and anyway we divorced when Leah was still at primary school. Although I had the right to see her regularly, she had custody of our daughter – who grew up to be a tart, just like her mother."

"So she left you for another man?" said Rachel Allen.

Morgan paused. "Let's say we both went our separate ways."

"But you have remarried?" said Matthews.

"Well, they say once bitten, twice shy but, yes, I did remarry. Quite recently. You've met my wife at the reception. She has been my secretary for several years."

"You're not close to your daughter then?"

"No." A brief show of disgust on his face left no room for doubt.

"May I ask then why you made serious allegations against a teacher at her school when she was a teenager even though by your own admission you had little contact with her?"

It was clear from Morgan's expression that the question was not one he had been expecting at all and he seemed at a loss for words. Eventually he replied, "I heard rumours."

Matthews could barely hold back his disgust. "You heard rumours! You were prepared to destroy a man's reputation on the basis of rumours?"

Rachel Allen intervened, "From whom did you hear these rumours?"

"From her friend, Pippa Hendricks. Her father works for me and he mentioned to me in passing something his daughter had said. Morgan was getting irritable. "Look, what is this really all about? I'm sure it's not about an old incident with a paedophile teacher."

With difficulty, Matthews held his tongue, and motioned with his hand for Rachel to do likewise. He too wanted to get the interview back on track. "Robert Paisley. He was investigating your company."

"Really? Why?"

"He is — was, I mean — a private investigator looking particularly into your construction site in Topsham."

Morgan frowned. "Who was employing him?"

"I'm afraid we are not liberty to say," replied Matthews. "You didn't know?"

Morgan paused before replying, "I had heard from Hendricks that there was some bloke poking around trying to talk to the workers."

"Who are foreign." Matthews stated.

"Some are."

"Is Hendricks your foreman? Did he find out the name of this person?"

"Yes, he is one of my foremen, but I'm sure it wasn't Paisley he mentioned.

"That's probable. We think Paisley gave a false name, almost certainly the name of a council surveyor, who also happens to be your daughter's partner. Does Burgess ring a bell?"

"Possibly. I'd need to check."

"Can you confirm that all your workers are registered UK citizens?"

"My workers. But some of the work is contracted out, and I can't vouch for what arrangement the sub-contractors have in place."

"I presume you can provide us with a list of your sub-contractors?"

"Not off the top of my head but I can ask Kelly-Ann to send it on to you."

"Just one further question, can you confirm where you were on the Friday evening and Saturday morning the weekend before last?"

"You surely don't think I had anything to do with Paisley's death?"

Matthews thought Morgan's attempt at incredulity deflected the need to answer his question directly. "We have to check on all possibilities, however unlikely they may seem."

Morgan pointedly looked at his watch. "Will that be all?"

"For the time being."

Morgan didn't attempt to shake their hands again as the two detectives stood and made to leave.

Before they set out back to Exmouth, Matthews just slumped back in the car, brow furrowed and deep in thought for several minutes. Eventually he let out deep breath, "What was your impression of Morgan, Rachel?"

"Slippery customer, I'd say, sir. And spiteful too. All that business about accusing Brooks on the basis of a rumour from a third party."

"I agree. And he didn't really tell us much that we didn't already know."

"May I ask why you didn't mention the minibus or the body on the beach?"

"I wanted to leave him feeling confident that we didn't present any threat to him. I need to have something definite linking the body to that farm hideout. When we get that we'll be hitting him hard and I'll have a search warrant for his home and Sowton depot."

CHAPTER 19

Chris didn't return home that evening. Leah turned in early, emotionally drained by the day's events. Next morning she awoke alone in her bed, and she soon noticed that he hadn't even taken to the sofa in the lounge. She was worried, more for his safety than his threat to leave her, since he would have been in no fit state to drive. He could be in hospital after an accident, or sobering up in the police station.

His mobile went to voicemail. She went through the motions of getting Stella, who was unusually subdued, ready for school and herself prepared for work, while turning all kinds of possibilities over in her head. She couldn't think of any obvious place that Chris would have spent the night.

At work, when there were no customers, she tried a couple of more times without success to contact Chris on his mobile. She also checked with Accident and Emergency at the Royal Devon and Exeter Hospital and, to her relief, heard that no-one by the name of Chris Burgess had been admitted. She thought about contacting the police to see if he'd been held overnight for drunk driving but assumed that he would have been released anyway and more than likely would have rung her for a lift. Business picked up as the morning progressed requiring her to put aside her worries and concentrate on her customers' requirements. Fortunately, the owner, Miriam Roseberry, was due to come in after lunch for one of her stints 'to keep in touch' as she said, enabling Leah to collect Stella from school.

Having parked nearby, Leah stood by the school gates with other parents waiting for the children to come out. The school had a policy of releasing one year group at a time, with a couple of minutes gap, to avoid unnecessary congestion. Stella's reception class would be first. But when the youngsters came out, laughing, chatting and hurrying to their mother, or in a few instances, their father, Stella was not among them. Worried, Leah approached the supervising teacher, whom she did not recognise. "My daughter, Stella, she's not here! Have you seen her?"

"I'm sorry, Mrs ... er?"

"Morgan. My daughter is Stella Burgess-Morgan"

"I'm sorry, Mrs Morgan, I don't know her. I'm on supply here as her regular teacher called in sick. I've had the same children in the class all day. No-one has left. Perhaps have a word with the school secretary?"

"I will, thank you." Leah was close to panicking but strode off towards the school building to speak to the secretary and the headmistress, her mother. The next group of children were now leaving.

"Mrs Morgan," the school secretary recognised her, "Can I help you?"

"My daughter, Stella, I brought her in this morning but she's wasn't with her class just now when I came to collect her. Have you seen her?"

"I think she was here first thing his morning, little young lass who was crying and wanted to see the Headmistress. But I haven't seen her since."

"Can I see the Head? Mrs Samuelson is Stella's grandmother."

"I'm afraid Mrs Samuelson is not here. She left early today."

"What shall I do? What shall I do!" Leah cried, "Where is she?"

The secretary offered to ring the Headmistress but Leah rushed outside into the school playground, grabbing her mobile phone and punching in her partner's number. A brief respite in her distress when Chris answered.

"Chris! Have you got her?"

"Leah? What's up?"

"Stella. Have you taken her?" Leah demanded.

"No of course not! You usually pick her up on Thursdays."

"But you said last night that you were going to take her!"

"I was drunk and, I'm sorry, I lost it. I haven't taken Stella."

"What am I going to do!" Leah cried, frantically, "She's not here!"

Chris tried to keep his voice calm. "Have you spoken to her teacher or your mother?"

"It's a supply teacher. She hasn't seen Stella, and my mother isn't here!"

"Okay, look, go back home and I'll be with you as soon as I can. I'm leaving now."

* * *

Chris arrived home just as Leah was getting out of her car.

"What have you done with her?" Leah flared up.

"Nothing. Just calm down and let's go inside." Chris made to give her his arm but she pushed him aside.

Leah fumbled with key and as soon as she opened the door she made straight for the telephone, "I must ring Lucy!" she cried.

As she was about to dial she realised the message tone was beeping. She pressed the buttons to listen.

"Hello, Leah, it's your mother. Please ring me back. I've got Stella with me."

Leah caught a her breath, and started dialling. She glanced at Chris and gave a brief nod

"What is it?" asked Chris.

"Stella's okay. She's with Mum."

"Oh Leah!" Denise Samuelson said. "You must have been worried. I've been trying to contact you but you weren't at work, or at home and I've not got your mobile number."

"What's happened?" Leah asked her mother.

"When Stella came into school today she didn't go to her class. She came directly to my office, crying. She was really upset. She said she'd heard you and Chris arguing and that he was going to take her away from you. I hoped she'd settle down after a while but she didn't want to go back to her friends in class even after lunch so I let her stay in my room and gave her some toys to play with. Unfortunately I had to leave early and she still resisted rejoining her class, so I let her come with me. I'm sorry, I assumed I'd be able to contact you to let you know, so I hadn't said anything to anybody else at the school."

"Mum, I'm so glad she's okay." Leah sighed with relief and looked at Chris, "We'll be right over. Both of us."

Hearing her comment, Chris said, "I'll drive." and Leah nodded assent.

Leah sat looking at the road ahead. Chris glanced at her and broke the silence between them. "I'm so sorry for losing my temper with you yesterday evening – and sorry for upsetting Stella." When Leah hadn't responded after a few seconds, he added, "I love you, Leah."

Leah spoke quietly, "I'm sorry, too, that I accused you of taking Stella." She paused for a moment. "I'm not having an affair with anyone else. I arranged to meet Mike Brooks to tell him that the DNA tests had confirmed he was Lucy's father. We've no intention of rekindling a relationship – not that there ever really was one. I'm happy with you, Chris."

"Does Lucy now know who her real dad is?"

"Yes. I shall be taking Lucy to meet Mike at his house on Saturday evening. I was going to ask you if you would like to come too."

Chris thought for a moment. "I think it would be better if it's just the two of you this time, but I'm happy to meet him at some future occasion."

"Where did you go last night? You'd obviously had a skinful and I was worried you'd had an accident."

"I spent all night in the car in the sea front car park in Budleigh. I knew I shouldn't be driving. I was going to walk back but I just fell asleep."

"Thank goodness you're safe."

* * *

Denise Samuelson lived in a modern detached house in Lympstone, only a short drive from the school in Budleigh Salterton where she was headmistress. After nearly eighteen years in the post she was looking forward to retirement in a couple of year's time. She had married Charles at the tender age of twenty after a whirlwind romance, and Leah was born soon afterwards.

They had been happy together at first, allowing Denise to complete her teacher training and give full motherly attention to her daughter. She had always suspected, however, that Charles had a roving eye and their marriage had foundered when he announced he was leaving her for some blue-eyed floozie with silicone enhanced boobs.

It had not been easy in practice being a single mother but with Leah of school age and attending the same school where she was teaching, she had coped with the situation. When Leah was old enough to move up to secondary school, Denise had married another teacher – like her, divorced, though childless, and several years her senior in age. While Leah had never taken to him as a substitute father, they had got on reasonably well together. Sadly, her new husband had contracted terminal pancreatic cancer and left her a widow some five years ago.

Leah's mother had already opened the front door by the time Leah and Chris had got out of the car, which he had parked in the drive. Stella came running over, tears and smiles mingling on her face, and beamed when Leah scooped her up for a big cuddle. Chris gave Stella a similar greeting.

In his arms she then frowned and said, "Daddy, you're not going away, are you?"

"No, sweetie, I'm not. Mummy and I had a misunderstanding but it's all cleared up now. We both love you."

They accepted the offer from Denise to stay for

supper. Over the meal, Leah brought her mother up to date on all the events concerning Mike Brooks and Robert Paisley.

"I've never trusted Robert," said Denise. "When we met up – which thankfully wasn't very often – he always wanted to be in charge, and was inclined to bully Leah if she didn't agree with him. My sister used to despair of him as he grew up into a teenager."

CHAPTER 20

Matthews looked up as Rachel Allen knocked on his door and entered the office. "Make my day, Rachel, tell me we've got some good news. We seem to be getting nowhere in finding Paisley's killer."

"Not sure about Paisley, sir, but we have had a sighting of the minibus."

"Oh yes? Where?"

"In the back lanes near Holcombe Rogus. Patrol car met it coming the other way, and pulled in to let it pass. Only realised afterwards that it was on the search list."

"Right, then we'll ask for increased observation in that area, and for the vehicle to be discreetly followed if found. With a bit of luck it may lead us to some new construction site or billet for foreign workers. We may need to liaise with the Somerset police as that village is near the county boundary. Anything else?"

"No report back yet from forensics on that farm."

"Well, it is early days, and there was quite a lot to cover."

"One strange thing, though, sir. Fingerprints from Paisley's bed frame."

Matthews perked up. "Have we got an identity?"

"Yes, sir. They belong to Simon Brooks. The constable who works from here."

"What on earth ... ?" Matthews said, puzzled. "How the devil did his prints end up there, and probably with Paisley's USB stick.?"

"He had met Paisley, sir." Rachel said, "At the Rolle Arms."

"Ye..es. But I can't imagine Paisley gave him the stick voluntarily, given the circumstances."

"He could have accidentally dropped it."

"Hmm. Still doesn't explain how it then got into Paisley's flat."

They both stayed silent in thought for a minute.

Rachel thought of a possibility. "Sir, there was a police constable on duty outside Paisley's flat waiting for forensics while we went to the Bicton Inn. Could have been Brooks."

"Good thinking. Can't say as I noticed. Check on that, will you, before we have a word with the young man."

"Anything else, sir?"

"Yes. I think we need to go back and check all the CCTV coverage for the roads to and from East Budleigh from, say, eleven o'clock that Friday evening, to eight o'clock the following morning for any of the vehicles connected to anyone we've been investigating, so," Matthews counted off on his fingers, "Paisley's, Mike Brooks', Leah Morgan's,

Charles Morgan's car and minibus – and add in Miriam Roseberry, Denise Samuelson, Chris Burgess Simon Brooks, and Dennis Inwood to cover all possibilities. And, if Celia Telling owns a car, check her as well" Matthews saw Rachel raise her eyes to the ceiling at the implications of all that extra work. "Get young Watkins to help you."

Rachel left the office and hurried over to speak to D.C. Watkins. She indicated Matthews office, explained to him what was required, "I've got another matter to attend to first but I'll be back to help, if you can get things started,"

Some twenty minutes or so later, Rachel returned to her superior's office.

"Bingo, sir! It was Brooks on duty outside Paisley's flat. He's out on patrol at the moment but he's been asked to report back here to you as soon as possible."

The rest of the morning had passed before P.C. Brooks stood before Matthews, and Allen, who had been asked to join them.

"I'm sorry, sir, we had a traffic incident which took some time to resolve."

"That's okay, Constable Brooks." Matthews got straight to the point, "Can you explain how your fingerprints came to be found on the bed frame in Paisley's flat, next to where the USB stick was tucked? The stick, incidentally, is free from any prints."

Simon Brooks could not meet Matthews' eyes,

and he blushed as he sought to explain. "I did put the stick there, sir."

"Why?"

"I had intended to hand it in, sir, but then I found myself sent to guard Paisley's flat I thought it was a good opportunity to hide it somewhere where I was pretty certain it would be discovered."

"For what purpose?"

"I thought that the information on the stick about his investigation into the construction company was very important and would probably lead to the persons who had broken into to his home." Brooks was beginning to sound more relaxed.

"You obviously studied the content of the stick then?"

"Yes."

"And wiped it clean of your prints – and any others including Paisley's?"

"Yes. I admit that wasn't very sensible."

"Did you also wipe the stick free of any reference to Morgan? You see, on the laptop there is a folder labelled Morgan but nothing at all on the stick."

P.C. Brooks looked flustered again. "I ... I ..." He took a deep breath. "I found that Paisley was investigating a supposed stalking of Leah Morgan's daughter, Lucy. Though he wasn't yet certain, he suspected my younger brother, Steven." Brooks grimaced. "I couldn't let that become public. Steven has always been very shy where girls are concerned. I thought it best to have a quiet word with him myself."

Matthews considered this latest revelation thoughtfully. "Have you spoken to him yet?"

"No sir, I haven't really had the opportunity yet. I have been wondering what to say." Nervously, he asked, "Am I going to be in trouble, sir?"

"In all honesty, at this stage I'm not sure, but I can't rule it out." Matthews stroked his chin. "I think you've been incredibly foolish but you haven't actually withheld any vital evidence, and I can understand your concern about your brother, who as far as I can see, hasn't committed any crime. One point, however, how did you come into possession of the stick?"

"I found it at the Rolle Arms after we'd got rid of Paisley,"

Matthews looked at Rachel, who nodded, in acknowledgement that her theory had been verified.

"Why didn't you return it or hand it in to us?"

"I don't really know. I wasn't quite sure what to do with it, and as I said I didn't want Steven to be put at risk. It was only when I discovered Paisley was dead that I thought it would be relevant to your investigations."

"Okay, P.C. Brooks. We'll leave it there at the moment. I suggest you speak with your brother without further delay. It is possible we may want to speak with him or with you again. You're free to go."

"Thank you, sir – and ma'am."

"Impressions, Rachel?" said Matthews when the constable had left.

"Rather wet behind the ears, I think, but he appears honest."

"Hmm, you're probably right. I've got that little niggling feeling again that there's something I've missed. Hopefully it will come back to me."

CHAPTER 21

Leah had let Lucy drive the three or four miles from her Budleigh flat to Mike's house in Otterton.

"Are you feeling nervous?" Leah asked as they walked up the path.

"A little," Lucy replied.

Before Leah had even rung the bell the front door opened and Mike stood there, arms wide ready to great them. "Leah," he said, "so glad you could come!" He gave her a hug. "And Lucy too!" He turned to her and smiled.

Lucy wasn't sure how to react. She blushed, then after a few moments embraced him. "Hello .... Dad."

Mike chuckled. "Yes, it seems I am your dad, but I'm quite happy for you to call me Mike if you feel more comfortable with that. I understand you have a very supportive father figure at home."

"Thank you .... Mike." Lucy was tongue-tied for further comment.

"Anyhow come on in and sit down. I've put the kettle on – or would you prefer something stronger? A wine or brandy?"

Leah looked at her daughter and raised an eyebrow, inviting her to make the choice.

"I'd quite like a glass of wine," said Lucy, "if that's okay with you, Mum?"

"I'll go along with that. Same for me, please. Red, for preference."

While Mike opened a cabinet and reached for a bottle and glasses, Lucy looked at the photograph of Mike with a teenage lad and a man probably some ten years or so older. All were formally dressed. The teenager seemed familiar.

"Me and my two sons , Steven and Simon – your half-brothers, I suppose," said Mike, handing Lucy a glass of Shiraz.

"I'm sure I recognise the younger son. Steven?" Lucy said.

Both Leah and Mike look surprised. "Where from?" her mother asked.

"In the shop, Mum," Lucy replied, "two or three weeks ago, I think. This young man came in to buy some flowers, for his mother he said. You were out the back making a cup of tea."

"The flowers would have been for her grave," said Mike, "for the anniversary of her death just over a year ago."

"I'm sorry to hear that," said Lucy.

"Happy release, really, "said Mike, "She had been suffering from advanced Alzheimer's. But now tell me a bit about yourself."

"I'm still in the sixth form at school and will be

taking my A levels next summer. And I help Mum in the shop when I can."

"What are you studying?"

"Art, history and English literature."

"University afterwards then?"

"Well, we'll see. Probably, but I haven't really made up my mind yet."

Leah was glad that Lucy seemed to be much more relaxed and happy to chat.

"What do Steven and Simon do," Lucy asked.

"Simon joined the police force. He's still a constable in uniform but he's hoping to move up to sergeant soon. Steven is, well, having a gap year. He had thought about teaching but I'm glad in a way that he's not following in my footsteps, as he's quite shy. I'm not sure he really knows what he wants to do but he earns a bit of cash playing in a band and has been working part-time at Exeter's Museum and Art Gallery. Actually, you'd probably get along well together as his degree was in Art History."

They chatted for a while longer, Leah trying to steer the topic away from schools as she didn't want Mike to start reminiscing in front of Lucy. She declined a top up of wine with the excuse that she had to drive, and Lucy also took her cue.

When they were ready to take their leave, Mike gave each of them another hug. "Thank you so much for coming. I've no intention of imposing myself on your life but you are always welcome to visit, and, Lucy, I'd love to know how from time to time how you are getting on."

It was still daylight when Leah dropped Lucy off along the sea front in Budleigh Salterton. "No need to take me to the door, I'll walk the rest. I could do with a breath of fresh air."

As Lucy approached her flat she glanced back along the road, and caught sight of a young man in a hoodie darting behind a bus shelter. Thinking that it might be the person who had been stalking her, she decided to confront him and turned back. On a fine June evening there were still many people out and about, so she didn't feel threatened. When he peeked out from behind the shelter, Lucy was almost on him, and caught hold of his shoulder as he turned to run.

Lucy pulled him round to face her. "What the hell are you up to, spying on ...." She then pulled up, in surprise. "Steven?"

He recoiled in shock, "How ... how do you know my name?"

"Just an hour or so ago I saw a photograph of you with your father and older brother."

"Wha .... what!" He stared at her open mouthed.

"It is you that has been stalking me these past few weeks?"

"No... no! Not stalking you. I just wanted to see you again." Steven mumbled the last comment.

"That would be after you came into the shop to buy some flowers?"

Steven looked up, brightly, "You remember me?"

Lucy was beginning to feel rather sorry for Steven who, she was sure, didn't present any threat whatsoever to her safety, particularly now he was aware of her contact with his father. "Steven, we need to both understand what's going on. I'm not going to invite you into my flat until that's sorted but would you like to join me for a coffee?" She indicated the cafe just across the road.

"I ... I... I'd love to, " Steven stuttered, "I ... I've never ..."

Lucy put her hand up, "Hold on, Steven, save it for a moment. let's get inside and sit down."

Lucy bought a large Americano for herself and a latte which Steven had asked for when Lucy offered to pay for both of them. They found a table for themselves in the corner well away from other customers.

"Right, now, Steven, tell me what this all about?"

"Thanks for the coffee ... er, I don't really know your name."

"I'm Lucy Morgan. My mother is manager of the florist shop."

Steven took a sip of his coffee, and just sat there thinking for a few moments. He then raised his head and looked at her, and said sheepishly. "I've never really had a girl friend, and you looked so beautiful."

Lucy couldn't help blushing. "That's very sweet of you."

"I really wanted to ask you out but I'm not very confident, and I thought you might make fun of me."

"Oh, Steven, you poor lad!" Lucy corrected

herself when she saw Steven's face cloud over. "I'm sorry, I didn't mean to sound patronising." She took his hand gently, "Listen, there is something important I need to tell you."

Steven looked up nervously.

"My mother and I were at your father's house earlier this evening, at his invitation. I have only just found out that my mother had a brief affair with your father when she was still at university. He is my father too – and you are my half-brother."

Steven looked miserable at hearing that news,

Lucy stood and gently raised Steven to his feet. She put her arms round him to give him a hug, and then kissed him. "We can't be, like, girl and boy friend together, but we can be friends – and I would be very happy with that."

"If we can see each other I will be happy to be your brother." Steven smiled, and hugged her again.

CHAPTER 22

Sunday morning Simon took the rare opportunity to have a lie in. No work shifts, and he'd been quite late getting home after a very pleasant evening in the company of his new girl friend. With just a couple of dates it was still early days in their relationship, and Simon thought the likelihood of them sleeping together was still some way off, though not too far in the future, he hoped.

He thought it would be a good opportunity to meet up for a chat with his brother, something he'd been meaning to do, but work and other commitments had taken priority. Quite possibly Steven would also not be an early riser on a Sunday, so Simon took a leisurely breakfast before calling his mobile.

Steven answered on the third ring.

"Hi, Steven, it's Simon here. Are you at Dad's or your flat?"

"I'm at my pad. I was in Budleigh until quite late."

"Fancy meeting up for a pie and a pint at lunchtime?"

""Yeah, that would be good. In Exmouth?"

"I'm easy. Or how about Lympstone? I'll take the train so I don't have to worry about drinking. The Swan's right next to the station."

"That's okay with me. I'll take my bike, though. See you there, say twelve thirty?"

As the pub was likely to be busy, Simon arrived early. He took a seat at an outside table, a gentle breeze complementing the sunshine to give a pleasant and comfortable temperature. "You look as if you could do with a drink," he said when his brother pedalled up, dismounted and propped his bike up against the wall. "I'll get a menu too."

Steven had always looked up to his older brother, who in turn had tried to give him whatever support he needed, particularly as he wasn't very good at standing up for himself in any kind of confrontation.

"Have you been doing any gigs recently?" Simon enquired as they waited for their meal to be served.

"A few here and there," Steven replied, "they're always on the lookout for a decent bass player."

"Do you get paid?" Simon knew that his brother showed the most confidence when he had his electric bass in his hands.

"Sometimes we get a few quid, other occasions it's a share of what's been collected in the hat or just free booze and grub."

They chatted casually over their meal. Steven

offered to get the next round of drinks, but Simon held up his hand, and said, "No, this is on me.

He returned and set the two brimming glasses onto the table. "I've got something I've been meaning to share with you," Simon began. "Something that has cropped up through work."

"Oh yes?" Steven said, intrigued.

"It seems that you were of interest in an investigation"

"What? Why?"

"You were suspected of stalking a teenage girl. Tell me it's not true, Steven."

Simon had expected his brother to be worried and was unprepared for the big smile that broke out across his face. "You're talking about Lucy Morgan?"

"Yes. How did you know?" It was Simon's turn to be intrigued.

"I admit I did follow her. Ever since I saw her in the florist's when I bought flowers for Mum's grave, I wanted to get to know her. Yesterday evening she caught me. We had a long chat." Steven paused, not sure how much his brother knew about the family connection. "She is my – our step-sister."

Simon nodded.

"You knew?" Steven asked.

"Only very recently. Dad told me."

"But how did you find out that I ... I was interested in her?"

"She told her mother – that's Leah Morgan – that

she thought someone was following or watching her, and she got someone to look into it."

"Not the police?"

"Then who?"

"Her cousin, Robert Paisley, who was a private investigator.

"Was?"

"He was found dead. Possibly a hit and run accident but it's being investigated."

"Are you involved?"

"No, I had come across him on one of my shifts when he was causing a disturbance at a pub. Tell me, Steven, did you ever meet him?"

"No, never."

"How do you feel about having a sister?" Simon asked, a twinkle in his eye.

"Um, happy I suppose. She's a lovely looking lass. I was really hoping she would be my girl-friend but I guess I'll have to settle for sibling."

CHAPTER 23

Matthews was hoping the start of a new week would see some significant developments into at least one of his current investigations but he wasn't really expecting to be showered with multiple reports covering various aspects of the two cases. While all would require detailed study, he scanned through each to decide which should be given priority. He put on one side CCTV reports from around the area that had identified vehicles belonging to some persons of interest in use in the hours either side of the estimated time of Paisley's death. A patrol officer had recently called in a sighting of the minibus, with the same registration number as the Topsham vehicle and apparently full of men, on the A38 south of Wellington. If a search was set up quickly there was a better than evens chance of finding the workers who had disappeared from Topsham. Being close to the Somerset border, however, liaison with Somerset police would be necessary. Matthews made a couple of quick phone calls to get things moving, then browsed the next report. Charles Morgan did indeed use several sub-contractors, all of which companies listed him as one of the directors. Definitely worth following up. Forensic evidence from the old farmhouse and stables had yielded a DNA match with that of the body recovered from the beach and fibres matching the clothing on the victim. Matthews felt that he had sufficient grounds to get a search warrant for Morgan's home office and his work depot in Sowton, and to question him under caution. Probably also his foreman, Hendricks.

Matthews opened his office door and called over to his sergeant who was just putting the phone down, "Rachel, could you come over here for a minute when you've finished."

She raised her hand in acknowledgement, and put the phone down.

"Anything important?" Matthews nodded towards her desk.

"Still chasing up a couple of private CCTVs that might be useful. So what's the plan for today, sir?"

"A busy day ahead, that's for sure. Firstly, I want you and D.C. Watkins to go over to the Topsham site and bring the foreman – Hendricks is his name – in for questioning. Don't put the wind up him, just ask him nicely for his help with some questions at the station, but don't take no for an answer."

Rachel smiled, "I'll use my charm."

"Then I'm sure he won't be able to resist you." Matthews chuckled. "Meanwhile I'm going to apply for a search warrant for Morgan's home and business premises."

* * *

As on their previous visit there was no sign of any questionable workers at the building site. The same man, however, was on the gate and recognised them. "You again!," he said gruffly, "What do you want this time?"

"We'd like to speak with the foreman, Mr Hendricks," said Rachel pleasantly.

"He's not here today."

"Oh really? Why's that?"

The gate man's eyes darted around, refusing the meet Rachel's. "Called in sick."

"Okay. Can you give us his address?" Suspecting that he was about to object or deny any knowledge, she added, "We can find out but it would save us time and hassle if you can help us. We won't let on that you provided the information."

After considering the matter for a minute, the gate man gave Rachel an address in the Withycombe area of Exmouth, "Keep your word. You didn't get this from me."

Rachel thanked him and made a brief call to her boss to update him on the situation.

"Back to Exmouth, Sarge ?" said D.C. Watkins, who was driving.

"Yes, but I have a feeling we won't find Hendricks at home."

Rachel's suspicions were soon verified. The overweight woman who answered the door to the attractive semi-detached house told them he was at work.

"Would that be at the depot in Sowton or the building development in Topsham?"

"One or the other, I guess."

"Thank you, Mrs Hendricks for your help." said Rachel and made to leave.

"It's Miss Hendricks. I'm his sister not his wife."

Rachel turned to her again, a thought having popped into her head. "Are you Pippa Hendricks?" Although her brown hair, tied up in a bob, was showing premature signs of greying, she could have been a similar age to Leah Morgan.

Her eyes opened wide in surprise. "Yes. How did you know?"

"Your name was mentioned in passing when we were talking to your former teacher, Mr Brooks, about another matter. He mentioned that you and Candy Archer were friends with Leah Morgan. Is that correct?"

Pippa gave a throaty chuckle, "Well, well, Basher Brooks! Yes, Candy, Leah and I were friends."

"Do you still see each other?"

"Candy, no. She got married to an Aussie and emigrated. I see Leah from time to time. Why are you asking?"

"Background really. She's not a suspect in our investigations. Tell me, what was Leah like as a teenager? We've heard suggestions that she had an eye for the boys."

"You could say that. Even had an eye for Basher but he wouldn't have touched her. At least not while she was a student at the school."

"But after?"

"Possibly. It wouldn't surprise me. She was quite a stunner – still is, quite. She's not wild like that nowadays, though. She seems to have found a good bloke to settle down with."

"Thanks very much for your help. You've confirmed quite a few things about Leah for us."

"You're welcome."

Rachel Allen debated whether to leave the trip to Exeter until after lunch but decided she'd probably be able to spend an uninterrupted afternoon in the office if she dealt with the matter sooner rather than later.

Surprisingly, the traffic was much lighter than she expected on the A376 to Exeter and, apart from a small queue heading for the services off junction 30 of the M5, there were no hold ups. Even the gates into the SiEmsCo depot in the Sowton trading estate were open and unmanned. As they wound their way towards where they assumed the office was located, Rachel saw a man emerge from the side of the single storey building, laden with an armful of paper, and head towards a smouldering brazier on the far side of the yard.

"Stop him!" Rachel yelled to Watkins, who put his foot down and their car shot forwards into the yard, blocking the man's path. Taken by surprise, his moments of indecision as to whether to run with his load to the brazier, dump the lot and run away or just stay where he was gave Rachel to chance to scramble out of the car almost before it had stopped, and confront him.

"Police! Stay where you are and put what you are carrying carefully onto the ground."

With the female officer approaching him and the driver now also following on foot, he felt he had little option but to comply.

"I am D.S. Allen," Rachel said, displaying her warrant card, "and my colleague is D.C. Watkins. We have a warrant to search these premises, starting with the office." Addressing Watkins, she pointed to the pile of documents, "Put these in the car before they get blown all over the place." She then turned her attention back to the person who had surrendered them. He stood looking at the ground with a surly expression on his face, hand thrust into the pockets of his jeans. His untidy long fair hair reached down to the shoulders of his check shirt. Rachel estimated that he was probably in his early forties, "Your name, sir, if you please."

"Hendricks." he said gruffly.

"Well, Mr Hendricks, am I right in thinking you were about to burn these papers?"

"Old stuff I've been clearing out. Nothing worth keeping." Hendricks grunted.

"We'll be the judge of that! Now, perhaps you would show us to the office where we will be conducting a thorough search. We will also be taking away any laptops or PCs for examination. And when we've done, we want you to come with us to Exmouth police station where we have some questions to ask you."

"Why do I have to go to Exmouth? Can't you ask me the questions here?"

"I'm afraid it's not my decision, sir. We'd like you to come voluntarily but I do have the authority to arrest you if you refuse."

"What? I've done nothing wrong. What's this all about anyway?"

"We are investigating a possible link between your firm's construction site at Topsham and two unexplained deaths. There may be nothing in it but coincidences like that usually raise suspicions. I understand you are the foreman at that site."

"Was. I'm due to start at another site tomorrow. And we haven't had any reports of trouble involving anyone in our workforces."

"In which case, I'm sure the matter will be cleared up quickly."

CHAPTER 24

Matthews asked the two uniformed officers to wait for five minutes in the patrol car which had parked out of direct view from Charles Morgan's house. The smile with which his wife prepared to greet a client quickly turned to a scowl as she recognised the person who appeared in the doorway.

"What do you want now?" she said curtly.

"I need to speak with Mr Morgan again," Matthews replied.

"He's ..."

"Now!" Matthews cut her off, sharply, "I see his car is outside, so please don't pretend that he's not here."

The door to the rear of the reception area opened and Charles Morgan strode in, looking first at Matthews and then his wife. "What's up, Kell?"

Matthews interceded before she could reply. "Mr. Morgan, I have here a warrant to search your premises ..."

"That's ridiculous!" Morgan shouted, "You have no reason to do so!"

"I'm afraid we have some very good reasons. Now please step aside."

Morgan glared as the other two police officers entered. "I forbid you to touch anything until I have spoken to my solicitor!"

"You would be well advised to contact your solicitor but we will begin the search with or without your co-operation. Your Sowton premises are also being searched. We will also want you to accompany us to the police station." Matthews gave Morgan a copy of the search warrant.

"You bloody pigs! You are not..."

Matthews interrupted, "Officers, please handcuff Mr Morgan and escort him to the car." He then faced Morgan who was red with anger, shouting and struggling, to no avail. "Mr. Morgan I am arresting you for obstructing the police in their investigation." He then recited the usual caution informing him of his rights to silence and possible consequences.

Kelly-Ann looked distraught. "Charles, what's this all about? What have you done?"

"Shut up, you stupid bitch," he snarled as he was led out of the door.

Kelly-Ann slumped in her chair, crying.

"I am sorry for your distress, Mrs Morgan, but we do have a job to do," said Matthews gently. "May I suggest you go into the main part of the house. You may want to ring someone to come and be with you. I'm afraid we are going to be some time, and it is quite probably that we may keep your husband at least overnight at the station. He will be able to call his solicitor but if you do know who that is likely to be then you may wish to inform him of what is happening. "

Kelly-Ann nodded. "Thank you," she said quietly.

"I should tell you that it is possible that we may need to talk to you later, depending on where our investigations take us. Now I'm going to call for some more assistance in my search. In the meantime, your husband will be taken to Exmouth Police Station where I will be questioning him later."

"Can I see him?"

"I'm afraid that won't be possible today. We will keep you informed."

Matthews began searching the single filing cabinet in the reception area, though he suspected anything important would be secured away in Morgan's office or somewhere else less obvious. He asked Kelly-Ann for keys to any locked drawers or cabinets. When his back-up team arrived half an hour later, he debated whether to stay longer or head back to the station to catch up on other developments and prepare to interview Morgan. He decided to check first with his sergeant to see what progress she had made.

"I was just going to ring you, sir," Rachel Allen answered his call. "We have Hendricks in custody. He was just about to burn some documents which I'm sure you'll find very interesting. Damning proof of using illegal workers. And we haven't had time to go through the rest of the stuff or the laptop. "

"Well done, Rachel! Are you back at the station?"

"Just arrived."

'I'll see you there shortly. By the way, Charles Morgan will be arriving soon. Keep Hendricks and him well apart."

***

A smartly dressed portly gentlemen approached Matthews as soon as he had entered the station. "Inspector, I demand that you release Mr Morgan without further delay. It is totally unacceptable that he was brought here in handcuffs like a common criminal for merely expressing his opinion!" he said haughtily. "I shall be reporting this matter to your superiors!"

Matthews raised his eyebrows and spoke calmly, "And you are?"

"Clive Ostwald-Bannister, his solicitor."

"Have you spoken to your client, sir?"

"Yes, of course!"

"Very well, Mr Ostwald-Bannister, you may wish to speak to him again. He was brought here for obstructing myself and my officers in implementing a search warrant for his premises. I will be interviewing him shortly and may well be arresting him for other more serious offences. Now, if you don't mind, I have some reports to check first."

"I ... I ... I object!" the solicitor spluttered, as Matthews turned and walked away towards his office.

Matthews called for an update from D.S. Allen and other officers who were involved in the latest investigations. Rachel reported that the papers so far recovered and examined from SiEmsCo Sowton depot showed clearly that illegal immigrants had been employed or, more likely, compelled to work for just basic food and lodging, at Topsham and other sites. The minibus carrying the workers had been intercepted at Wellington by the Avon and Somerset police. The driver and gangmaster were being held at Taunton Police Station, while the workers were being looked after temporarily at a community centre until an interpreter was brought in to assist with their questioning. However, the body recovered from the sea was recognised by several of them as one of their group, from a photograph sent to Taunton from Exmouth.

"We also have sightings of some vehicles of interest on the evening before and the morning of Robert Paisley's demise," said Matthews, "though, unlike the body on the beach, we can't as yet link his death to Morgan's company. His car was seen on the A3052 Exeter to Sidford road late on the Friday evening. Paisley's VW was heading out of Budleigh towards East Budleigh about 8 pm that same day. I think it's unlikely that they met. Any questions or other points?"

No-one volunteered to add anything else.

"Right, we will arrange for the minibus driver and his sidekick to be transferred here, and we'll get someone to talk to the foreign workers. In the meantime, I'm going to have a word with Hendricks before dealing with Morgan. Rachel, would you please join me?"

Hendricks was reluctant to make direct contact with the two detectives. He took the seat when invited to do so.

"Mr Hendricks, we will be interviewing you under caution but I understand you haven't asked for a solicitor." Matthews then recited the full caution.

"I haven't done anything wrong so I don't need one."

"Well, we'll see. I would advise you to be represented but it's your choice."

"I don't need one," Hendricks repeated.

"Okay, for the record," Matthews said, indicating the recording device, "please state that you have declined to have legal representation."

When Hendricks had complied, Matthews continued. "You were about to destroy some documents when my sergeant arrived. Why?"

"They were old stuff. I was having a clear out. As I told her." Hendricks nodded towards Rachel.

"Were you told to clear the stuff?"

Hendricks shrugged. "No, I had some spare time and I had put off the job for a while."

"Now think very carefully about that, Mr Hendricks. If you were acting on your own initiative then it implies you knew what was in the documents, and were seeking to destroy evidence that could prove your complicity in using illegal immigrant workers. And you would be charged with that offence."

Hendricks eyes were now darting all around the room, seeking some escape from his predicament. "I swear I didn't know what was in the documents."

"Oh come, come, Mr Hendricks! You don't expect us to believe that you just grabbed papers at random to burn. Now I'll ask you one more time. Did you know what was in the documents?"

"Yes," Hendricks whispered.

"Louder, please."

"Yes, I knew."

"And was that your own decision to destroy them? Bear in mind that you will be admitting to responsibility for an illegal act."

"No."

"So by whom were you instructed?"

"My boss."

"That would be Charles Morgan?"

"Yes." Hendricks gave up all signs of pretence. "He rang me at home. Told me not to go to Topsham but straight to Sowton. Tell the bloke in the office there to go home, and to destroy all the documents in certain marked folders in the locked cabinet. He told me where to find the key." Hendricks grimaced. "I suppose I should have burnt them as soon as I found them – you would then have had very little to go on – but I decided to collect everything together and make one trip to the fire. Took me a long time and the latter stuff really was old hat."

"I believe you've known Charles Morgan for a long time?"

"Most of my working life, He's been good to me." Hendricks looked utterly dejected at having split on his employer.

"So I would be correct in assuming that you knew there was something dodgy about having so many foreign workers."

"I suppose so. But we've never had any trouble before. He pays me well and they work hard."

"Did you know that one of the workers had been killed?"

Hendricks gave the question some thought before replying. "Not for sure, but I was surprised when he didn't turn up with the rest of the crew. And then the bus didn't turn up at all. I was told that they had been reassigned to a more urgent job, and I'd be getting some replacements from the local job centre."

"And what about Robert Paisley?"

Hendricks looked puzzled. "Who?"

"He was investigating the foreign workers issue. He might have used the name Burgess.

"Yes, he did come round one day. Said he was a council surveyor."

"He was found dead."

"I know nothing about that."

Matthews glanced at Rachel then addressed

Hendricks again. "I think we are finished for now. Thank you for your co-operation."

"What happens now?" Hendricks said, confusion showing in his face, "Am I free to go?"

"Yes for the time being, but please stay in the area. It is probable that we will need to speak to you again and I can't rule out the possibility that you will face criminal charges. However, your assistance in this enquiry would be taken into account. In the meantime please avoid all contact with Charles Morgan and his company."

Hendricks let out a great sigh of relief.

When he had been escorted out of the room, Rachel turned to her boss and said, "Now for the big one, sir?"

"Yes, but I'm going to keep it short. We need some time to examine the rest of the material collected from his office and works depot, and also see what the minibus crew can deliver."

Ten minutes later Charles Morgan was brought to the interview room, accompanied by his solicitor, who immediately spoke up, "I hope we can bring matters to a swift conclusion. My client has already been waiting here too long."

"Indeed, Mr Ostwald-Bannister, I will be brief. Please take a seat, gentlemen."

Morgan glared at Matthews, who shuffled some papers on the table, and then addressed them.

"Mr Morgan, when we interviewed you previously, you claimed that your subcontractors may use foreign labour, and as such you would not be responsible for checking on their status. Is that correct?"

"Yes, that is correct," Morgan answered confidently.

"We have looked into the sub-contractors you use. You are a named director in all of them."

Ostwald-Bannister looked sharply at his client.

"Charles Morgan, I am further arresting you on suspicion of the employment of illegal immigrants. You do not have to say anything ... "

Morgan interrupted angrily, "That's ridiculous! I ..."

"Shut up, Charles!" his solicitor said, putting his hand on his client's arm.

Morgan brushed his hand away, and yelled, "How dare you! I pay you through the nose to represent me, not insult me!"

"Charles, I am representing you and telling you for your own good to hold your tongue until we've heard what D.I. Matthews has to say, and we have had a chance to talk in private. If you can't accept that, I'm walking out of here now and you can find someone else. I'll be sending you my bill."

Morgan looked as if he was going to continue his ranting but eventually lowered his head, and muttered, "Very well."

Matthews regarded them both, keeping a grin off his face with difficulty. "Well, gentlemen, I shall start again," he said calmly and went through all the formal warning as he had done earlier in the day then added, "I am also arresting you on the suspicion of complicity in the murder of one of your foreign workers and of the private investigator Robert Paisley."

Both solicitor and client were clearly unprepared for such a serious allegation and remained speechless. Ostwald-Bannister was the first to gather his wits but before he could say anything, Matthews spoke again. "Before you raise the matter of bail, Mr Ostwald-Bannister, let me say that in view of the seriousness of the charges, your client will remain in custody here overnight, and we shall continue the interview tomorrow morning. That is all for now."

The solicitor was unsure whether to speak to his client before he was escorted back to the cells or raise objections. Matthews gathered his papers together and stood, ready to terminate the meeting. "Mr. Ostwald-Bannister, you will be able to see your client tomorrow morning before we speak to him again. Shall we say nine o'clock?"

"Fine," Ostwald-Bannister said, in a gruff voice which implied it was anything but fine.

"Well, Rachel," Matthews said, when the solicitor had left, "I think we've had a useful day."

"You've certainly rattled Morgan's cage, sir. I doubt if he'll sleep well tonight."

"I think it's unlikely that we'll have enough evidence to tie him to the death of the worker or of Paisley, but there's no way he'll wriggle out of the illegal immigrants matter. By the way, your efforts on the CCTV coverage showed Paisley heading out from Exmouth towards Budleigh on the evening prior to his death, and also, oddly, Simon Brook's car leaving Exmouth soon after five o'clock on the Saturday morning in the direction of Woodbury, and returning just over an hour later. He turned up for his shift at the normal time. I'd like you to check the information on Paisley's USB stick again and also the date of the altercation at the Rolle Arms that Brooks dealt with."

"Will do. Er, sir, do you want me to do it now or can I leave it to the morning?"

"The morning's fine. Get some rest!"

CHAPTER 25

There was a real buzz in the station the following morning, with the discovery of new evidence. The fingerprints on Paisley's laptop were found to be those of the minibus driver and blood traces found in the minibus proved to come from the dead foreign worker. At least two of the workers had also described seeing their colleague being severely beaten by the driver and the gangmaster at the cottage – a warning what would happen if any others of them tried to escape. As a result the driver and gangmaster had been charged with murder. While removing Charles Morgan from direct involvement in that death, it gave little credibility to his claim to know nothing about the illegal practices in his company. After a long discussion with Morgan's solicitor, Matthews was prepared not to object to the granting of bail only if and when he was no longer a suspect on Paisley's death.

With interviews, discussions and consideration of the latest evidence, it was late morning before

Matthews had the opportunity to ask his sergeant whether she had found anything of interest from the task he had given her.

"I couldn't find anything that raised questions in Paisley's notes, sir, nor in the report by P.C. Brooks of the pub bust-up, However the last dated entry on the USB files was after the incident at the pub."

"Really?" said Matthews. " Well done, Rachel, I knew there was something that was bugging me about that young copper. Obviously Paisley must still have had the stick when he left the pub."

"And Brooks must have somehow acquired it later?"

"Yes, indeed. And with his very early morning jaunt on that Saturday, he's got some explaining to do. Wherever he is, get him to my office as soon as possible!"

Matthews decided to begin gently. "Simon Brooks, you have already given us some help in our investigation into the death of Robert Paisley and information on his USB has already led to charges involving another death and use of illegal immigrant labour."

Simon Brooks visibly relaxed until the detective inspector continued. "However, we would like you to explain how the date on which you claim to have found the stick precedes the last dated entry on the documents it contains."

Matthews gave Brooks a few moments to consider his query, and then added. "We would also like you to tell us where you were between five o'clock and seven o'clock on the morning that Paisley's body was found by your father. We have CCTV of your car leaving Exmouth and returning during those two hours."

Simon rested his right hand on his forehead, grimaced, and took a deep breath. "I had a phone call from Celia Telling."

Matthews eyes shot up in surprise, "Why would she ring you, and so early?"

"We have been seeing each other, ever since I met her that evening at the Rolle Arms. Nothing serious yet but we get on well together and enjoy each other's company."

"Ye..es. So?"

"She was desperate for help. She thought she had knocked Paisley off her bike and killed him. She ... "

"Hang on there, Simon, you're not making sense. She knocked him off her bike?"

"Sorry, sir, I'll need to give you some background, which Celia told me subsequently. Paisley had accosted her as she returned home late Friday evening after working at the Rolle. He dragged her indoors and assaulted her. She said he was roaring drunk. Some time later he fell asleep and she managed to escape from his arms. She grabbed his keys and her mobile phone. She intended to get out of the house, and phone the police. Unfortunately he had woken up and made to grab her as she opened the front door. She told him the police were already on their way and threatened to throw away his car keys. Paisley seized her bike and pedalled off down the lane. Celia wanted her bike back and ran to the car park where she thought Paisley's car might be. She followed him some distance behind and caught up with him. He toppled over and fell. She thought she must have struck the cycle. She saw that he was bleeding from his head. He wasn't moving. She thought he was dead. That was when she rang me."

Matthews sat with his brow furrowed. "I'm going to leave you here for a couple of minutes. There is something I need to discuss with my sergeant." With a toss of his head he indicated to Rachel to follow him from the room.

"Well, Rachel, I'd be hard put to come up with an explanation as weird as that, but I have that feeling that's he's not making it up. It may even fit your theory of Paisley's car ending up at Woodbury Castle with a bike. What was your impression of him?"

"His account fits the known facts, I suppose. It would also let Charles Morgan off the hook."

"We need to get Celia in here as soon as possible, before young Brooks can speak to her again. It's possible that they may already have cooked up a mutually supportive statement and if her account is virtually identical then I shall be very suspicious as to its truthfulness, but we shall see. Celia should still be at the pub, so get Watkins to collect her then join me again with Brooks "

Matthews went over the details of Simon's

statement so far while waiting for Rachel to return.

"Okay, Simon, we are now at the point, I believe, at which you received the phone call."

"That's right, sir."

"Now tell me what happened next. What did you advise her to do?"

"I suggested she removed all documents from his pockets and any other items that might aid his identification. That, actually, included the USB stick. She found it. I told her to load her bike into the back of his car and drive it to Woodbury Castle car park, and I'd meet her there."

"Why didn't you tell her to call the police – or call it in yourself?"

"Until I'd had a chance to talk to her myself, I didn't know whether she had killed him at all, or if so, whether deliberately or accidentally. She could face a charge of manslaughter or murder and with only her word as to what really happened. I couldn't bear the thought of that, so I tried to, well, buy us a little time. I was going to report it, anonymously, when I got back to Exmouth. I didn't really expect my dad to be trundling along that lane so soon after she'd left the scene.

"And you've wasted a considerable amount of police time while we were chasing our tails!" Matthews said sharply. "Why for Christ's sake couldn't you have told us sooner!"

"I'm sorry, sir. It never seemed quite the right time."

"Humph! So tell us what happened next!"

"Celia was already at Woodbury Castle when I arrived. She'd parked Paisley's VW well out of sight of the main road. She gave me the USB stick and I told her to leave all Paisley's documents on the front seat of his car. I helped her get her bike out of the car. By the way, I could see no damage to the bike or to the car from a possible collision between them. You'll still be able to check the bike. I told her to cycle back home but not by the way she had come."

"And then you set the car on fire?"

"Yes. Again to delay identification and destroy any evidence of Celia having been in the car. I'd brought a can of petrol with me. Laid a short trail to give me time to get back to my car and drive away."

When Matthews didn't comment and just sat there thinking, with his arms folded, eyes, almost closed, Simon glanced at both officers and said, obviously worried, "What will happen to me now, sir – and to Celia?"

Matthews held his eye, "At the very least you are going to be charged with gross professional misconduct. You've certainly caused us a lot of unnecessary work although I do understand the reason for your actions, however inadvisable they were. As to any further action it may depend on what Celia has to say. She's being brought into the station. I will need to discuss the matter with our superintendent. In the meantime you are suspended from duty until further notice.

However, whatever disciplinary action is taken against you, you would be well advised to get professional support. That's all I have to say at the moment but I'd like you to remain in the station. I suggest you get yourself a coffee in the canteen and wait till I call you."

"Thank you, sir."

When Simon had left, Matthews suggested to his sergeant that they both take a break before interviewing Celia. "I'm really not sure what to do about Simon Brooks," he said. "I cannot just ignore, shall we say, his professional indiscretions."

"I feel some sympathy for him being caught in a situation where he had to make a choice between his personal and professional life." said Rachel.

"I agree with you, but that is something which all of us may be called to face at some point in our life."

Celia appeared very nervous as she was led into the interview room. Matthews tried to put her at ease. "Please take a seat, Miss Telling. You have already spoken to us about the incident at the Rolle Arms with your former boy friend, Robert Paisley, but we have some further questions that may help us understand how he came to meet his death. We are not interviewing you under caution but if you do feel uncomfortable with the questions and wish to have a solicitor present then please say so. We would, however, like to record the interview, if you have no objection."

Celia nodded.

"We are particularly interested in the period between eleven o'clock on the Friday evening and six o'clock the following morning, around the time his body was discovered. We have reason to believe that he came to your house. Is that correct?"

"Yes," Celia said quietly.

"Please tell us what happened."

"I had left work about 11.15 and cycled back to my house in the village centre. I was just opening my front door when I was grabbed from behind, and he put his hand over my mouth to stop me screaming."

"You knew it was Paisley?"

"I was pretty sure, and I knew he'd been drinking. I could smell the alcohol on his breath when he spoke."

"Had he been at the Rolle Arms?"

"No way. Dennis would have thrown him out. He might have been at the Sir Walter Raleigh in the village. He could have been keeping a look out for me from there – or from his car in the car park. He'd still got his keys in his hand and they were pressing into my back. He'd obviously found out my address."

"We can check on that pub. What did Paisley say?"

"He was quite gentle at first. He pleaded with me to let him stay the night and said 'They're after me and they know where I live'."

Matthews and Allen looked at each other. "Did he say who 'they' were?" Matthews asked.

"No. And I didn't believe him and told him to f... off. His mood changed so quickly, and he became violent and abusive. Accused me of being a whore and shagging Inwood – something I would never do. He then forced me inside and into my bedroom. He .... he raped me." Celia looked close to tears.

Matthews remembered that Simon Brooks had only mentioned assault. Perhaps Celia hadn't told him. "Do you want to take a short break?" he asked kindly.

"No, I'll be okay," she replied, wiping her eyes with a small handkerchief she had pulled out of her sleeve.

"What happened next?"

"He fell asleep on top of me. I was trapped and couldn't move. Eventually, probably an hour or so later, he rolled over and I was able to wriggle out. I put on my clothes and crept downstairs. I wanted to get out of the house and call the police. I found my mobile and picked up his keys where he'd dropped them on the floor in the hallway. I was just going out of the front door when I heard him hurtling down the stairs. He lunged at me but I managed to get outside and push the door in his face. When he opened it I held up my phone and told him the police were on their way. "

"Which they weren't," said Rachel.

"No, I didn't have time. I also held his keys above a drain and threatened to drop them if he came any nearer to me. He then grabbed my bike, pushed me aside and pedalled like mad to the lane out of the village. I was pretty pissed off that he'd taken my bike. I'd only bought it recently and I didn't want to find it damaged and chucked away. I thought his VW might be in the car park, so when I found it, I set off to follow him."

"What did you intend to do when you caught up with him?" Matthews asked.

"I don't know. I wasn't really thinking. Keep following him until we got somewhere with other people around and give him his keys in exchange for my bike perhaps. I don't know."

"What would you have done if he had stopped and come towards you? You wouldn't have been able to turn around, and reversing along a narrow lane is tricky."

Celia shrugged her shoulders, and shook her head.

"But you did catch up with him, didn't you?"

"Sort of. He was just in front of me and I saw the bike wobble. Next thing he was flying through the air and collapsed on the ground. I don't think the car hit the bike, I didn't feel any bump, and there's no damage to my bike. There were some large potholes along that stretch so he might have hit one." Celia paused and took a deep breath. "I went over to him. He was lying there, not moving. He had a gash on his head and was bleeding. I thought he was dead."

"But you didn't touch him? Feel his neck for a pulse?"

"No. "

"Why didn't you call for an ambulance?"

"I was scared. I thought the police would come as well, and they'd arrest me for his murder."

"Did you kill him?"

"No! But I didn't think the police would believe me."

"So why did we find neither the car nor the bike at the scene?"

"I rang Simon – that's Simon Brooks, you know, the policeman who came the pub when Robert was making a nuisance. We ... we've been seeing each other since. I thought he could tell me what to do."

"And did he?"

"Yes. I'd woken him up. He told me to put my bike in the VW and drive up to Woodbury Castle car park, and he'd meet me there."

"Anything else?"

"Er, yes, he asked me to search Robert's pockets and take any wallet, driving licence or anything else that could identify him. I also found a small USB stick. I got to Woodbury Castle about five minutes before Simon."

"Go on."

"I gave him the documents and the USB stick – and car keys. He took my bike from the boot and told me to make my way home but not the way I came. He said he'd be in touch later. "

"Were you? "

"Not until Sunday, but he did ring me later on

Saturday to check I'd got home and was okay."

"Did he mention what he intended to do with Paisley's car?"

"No he didn't. And I didn't think of asking."

"I think that will be all for now, Miss Telling. Thank you for your co-operation." said Matthews.

"What's going to happen to me and Simon?"

"We'll need to check some things – the village pub, your bike, the pathologist's report to see if the injuries are consistent with what you have described. Simon is likely to face disciplinary action for his actions but if you are both telling the truth – and I stress, if, – then you may not face criminal charges. Is there anything else you want to tell me?"

"No, I don't think so. Oh, Robert will have some scratches on his face from when I struggled with him." Celia stood up ready to leave. "I'm expected back at the pub as soon as possible. Have I got to catch a bus?"

"No, Miss Telling, I will arrange for you to be driven back."

When she had left the interview room, Matthews asked Rachel to follow her. "I'm interested to see the reaction when Celia meets Simon." he said, smiling. "One more thing, Rachel. Take a photo of Paisley to the Sir Walter Raleigh pub and find out if he was there on that evening. Also check the road where we found the body for potholes."

CHAPTER 26

Simon eyes lit up when he saw Celia but, being still in uniform, he wasn't sure how to react. Celia had no reservations. She ran and flung her arms around him and buried her head against his shoulder, weeping softly.

"It's all right, Celia, it's all right" he said, stroking her hair gently.

"P.C. Brooks," Rachel said, relaying Matthews instructions to her, "please take Miss Telling home."

Simon acknowledged and, with his arm around her shoulder, led her outside to his car which he'd parked when he'd arrived for his shift that morning.

"Celia, I'm so sorry for what you've had to go through but I suspected that it would only be a matter of time before the truth came out."

"I know, Simon. And I'm so sorry that I've put your job at risk by asking you to help me. The detective inspector didn't mention your name at all when he was interviewing me, so I wasn't aware that he had spoken to you first."

"Matthews is a wily old bird but well respected for his honesty and fairness. I had no choice but to tell him what happened after you rang me but he could have used the CCTV image of Paisley heading towards Budleigh as a pretext for suggesting that he met up with you."

Celia took a deep breath. "Simon, there is something I told Inspector Matthews but I haven't told you. Robert raped me that night."

"Christ Almighty! If I'd have known I would have bloody well killed him!" Simon exclaimed, then took stock of what he'd just said. "It would have given you a motive!"

"I didn't kill him, Simon. And I think Matthews believed me. He hasn't arrested me."

"Well, let's hope he doesn't change his mind."

As they approached the Rolle Arms, Celia called out "What's that!"

"It's an ambulance!" Simon replied, worried about a new crisis.

Simon pulled the car in to the side of the road a few yards behind the ambulance, and Celia quickly got out and rushed up to the paramedics, who were carrying someone out on a stretcher.

"What's happened, what's happened?" she cried.

"The landlord has had a heart attack," said one of the paramedics. "He's alive and I think he'll be okay but we've got to get him to hospital. Are you a relative?"

"No, I work here, behind the bar."

"You may want to have a word with the lady over there by the door. She called us."

"That's Jane, she's in charge of the kitchen" Celia rushed over to her.

Jane was very distressed but explained to Celia what had happened. "It was soon after you left," she said. "There were only a couple of people still in the bar, and I heard this chap yell out. Dennis had collapsed while gathering up empty glasses. I called 999. I suppose we'll have to close the pub this evening – but we've got a couple of tables reserved for dinner."

Celia put her arm round Jane to comfort her, and made a decision, "If you can manage the food, I can manage the bar. I can lock up at closing time."

Simon had joined Celia and had heard the last part of the conversation. "Would you like me to help? I'm not going to be needed back at the station this evening." he said, and added, under his breath, "If ever."

"Simon, would you? That's brilliant!" said Celia. She turned to Jane "How about it?"

Jane nodded.

"We'll ring the hospital later and find out about Dennis," said Celia, "He's a widower," she said to Simon. "He's got a son and daughter but one is in America and the other lives at the other end of the country. I'll see if I can find contact details and let them know."

CHAPTER 26

The landlord of the Sir Walter Raleigh did indeed recognise Robert Paisley. "He's not been in here recently but for a week or so he was in here virtually every night, and on the last occasion – that's probably the Friday you are interested in – he was here from about eight o'clock until closing time. Pretty tanked up by then."

"Thanks for your assistance," said Rachel.

She then drove out along Hayes lane and turned into the narrow road where the body was found. She didn't really need to look for potholes – her car registered several, particularly by the site of the incident. She got out of her car to survey the scene again to see whether anything could be at odds with Celia's account. In particular she considered the position of the boulder in relation to the road, and concluded that a body thrown from a bike toppling over to the left could have made contact with the stone.

Standing in the road she noticed a house in an elevated position a few hundred yards further up the road, though it became hidden from view as she moved towards the field entrance. All houses in the area were supposed to to have been visited by the police but she thought it worthwhile to double check whether the residents had seen anything.

As she pulled into the farmyard access to the house, a young man who had just climbed down from a tractor walked over to her car. Rachel wound down her window.

"Can I help you?" he asked.

"I'm Detective Sergeant Allen," she said, showing him her warrant card, "I'm following up the investigation of the death of a man whose body was found in the field gateway just down the road."

"Oh yes, I remember we did have an officer call round asking if we'd seen or heard anything. And we weren't able to access the field through that gate until the police removed their tape."

"I understand that someone heard a car accelerating along the road, is that right?"

"Yes, that would have been me. It was very early, about half five."

"Is there anything else you remember? Did you see the vehicle?"

"No, I didn't see it. From the sound I would guess it was a medium sized car." He paused a moment, "Come to think of it, I may have heard a car engine, idling, a few minutes earlier. Can't be sure, though."

"One more thing, the house up there," Rachel pointed, "It would be possible to see the road just where the body was found. Is that where you live?"

"No, I'm in the main farm house. That's a holiday let."

"Occupied at the time?" Rachel reminded him of the date.

"Should have been, but they left a day early, on the Friday evening. Sorry."

"That's a shame, but thanks anyway."

"Do you know who killed him?"

"We've a pretty good idea what happened."

* * *

When Rachel returned to the police station she saw Charles Morgan leaving with his solicitor.

Once inside, she said to Matthews, "You've let him go, then, sir?"

"Yes, we can't charge him with the death of Paisley nor link him directly to the beach body. The minibus driver will be charged with murder but despite encouragement he refuses to implicate Morgan. However, Morgan will be facing a prison sentence for his use of illegal immigrants."

"So I suppose we can thank Paisley for bringing the matter to our attention, unintentionally."

"Indeed. Anything to report back from East Budleigh?"

Rachel brought her boss up to date on her enquiries.

"I guess we can close that investigation as well. Insufficient evidence for a prosecution so in the unlikely event of something else turning up, we'll have to regard it as an accidental death."

"And what about P.C. Brooks?"

"Undoubtedly he will face charges of gross misconduct in impeding an investigation and possibly perverting the course of justice."

CHAPTER 27

Six months later

Mike Brooks rose from his seat. "I'd like to welcome you all here this evening to celebrate my birthday." He paused until the spontaneous clapping had ceased. "It's not a milestone one. I've still got a couple of years until my threescore and ten, but it is a very special occasion, to have my family – indeed my extended family – with me, and to celebrate the forthcoming addition of another. I'm delighted that Leah and her partner Chris could join us, and Lucy, whom they've brought up to be such a lovely lass."

Lucy blushed. Steven took her hand.

"And I'm sure that young Stella will grow up to be just as lovely."

Stella giggled and hugged her mother.

"My family will extend even further in the new year when Celia will become my daughter-in-law. I'd like you raise your glasses to Simon and Celia, and wish them good health and happy life together."

After the toast had been drunk and his guests

had sat down again. Mike continued his speech. "You are all probably aware that Simon, my son, resigned from the police force to take on the full-time management of this pub with his fiancée. That was at the request of the owner, Dennis Inwood, who was grateful for them keeping the pub going while he was in hospital." Mike raised his glass towards the man at the end of the table. "He still keeps a watchful eye on things, I think."

Dennis Inwood raised his glass in acknowledgement.

"I'll keep it short," Mike said. "I really appreciate Simon, Celia – and Dennis – for making the Rolle Arms available to us this evening. It seemed very appropriate. And I'd like to thank Jane, the chef, and the waitresses for providing such a wonderful supper.

Everyone clapped, then stood and clapped louder as Jane came out of the kitchen, followed by the four young waitresses.

"Not forgetting Miriam Roseberry, who has supplied all the floral decorations." After more applause, he concluded, "Enough of my prattle. Steven, my younger son, is expecting a few of his friends along later to entertain us with some music and song, but in the meantime make yourself comfortable, have a good gossip. And we'll cut the cake later."

The two dozen guests gradually rose from the long table that had been set up in the skittle alley and made their way into the cosy saloon bar area.

Mike hung back in the doorway and when Celia had finished helping the four waitresses to clear the tables, he walked over to her.

"Celia, can I have a word in private with you before we join the others? No need to worry," he said, seeing a look of concern on her face.

"Okay, Mike."

"I've not mentioned this before, not while Simon was with the police, and not until the investigation into Robert's death concluded that it had been accidental. Though I would have come forward if you had been charged."

Celia frowned, "Where are you going with this, Mike?"

"You didn't kill Robert. I did."

"What! What do you mean?"

"He was alive when I found him, badly injured from a head wound. But he opened his eyes and recognised me. I used to teach him. 'Basher', he mumbled, 'Pervert, like father like son.' He closed his eyes and whispered. I didn't catch all exactly what he said but it sounded like '... Celia tell... '. That's what I told the police. I didn't know you then but I think what he said was more likely to have been' I'll see Leah, tell her.' I did know Leah."

"So what did you do?"

"I was angry, He'd been a right bastard at school and he knew I'd been accused — falsely -of sexual misconduct with a student. That was Leah. I didn't know what he meant by 'like son'. On impulse I held my coat that I'd put over him over his nose and mouth until I felt his body go completely slack."

"God, what a mess!" Celia said. "Why are you telling me this now?"

"I didn't want you going through life with the thought that you might have killed him on your conscience. It's up to you whether you say anything to Simon."

"I don't think he needs to know. I'm not sure I did either but thank you, Mike, for trying to put my mind at rest. I had pretty much put it all behind me but I still have the occasional nightmare." Celia kissed him on the cheek, "Thank you – Dad-in-law to be!"

To the accompaniment of Steven's scratch band the guests sang happy birthday as Mike cut his birthday cake. He started working his way through the stack of unopened envelopes. "Well, well, well, there's a surprise, " he said, waving a card. In it was written, 'Best wishes, Des Matthews."

OTHER BOOKS BY COLIN ANDREWS

If you have enjoyed this novel you may like to try my previous books.

Fiction

A Matter of Degree (2011)

Humour and drama set in a teacher training college in mid-Wales during the early 1970's

Shattered Pretensions (2015)

Two separate stories in which the actions of a young teacher have devastating consequences

One Degree Over (2018)

More humour and drama in the sequel to *A Matter of Degree*, in the year following the graduation of the main characters.

Interface (2020)

A fast-moving thriller in which a journalist from Sydney investigates the abduction of his estranged father in London.

Captured Image (2022)

A murder set in Exeter with connections to a serious incident involving students at the university over forty years earlier.

Poems and short stories

Who Gives A Hoot (2014)

A collection, mostly amusing, of original songs, parodies, poems and short stories.

Non-fiction

Shepherd of the Downs (1979,1987, 2006)

The life and songs of Sussex shepherd, Michael Blann

Mumming in Devon Past and Present (2023)

Traditional mumming texts collected in Devon in the early part of the 20th century and modern texts in the same genre

All books are available through my website:
www.colinandrewsauthor.co.uk

ABOUT THE AUTHOR

Originally from Sussex, Colin moved to Devon with his wife in 1973. Since he took early retirement from his teaching post in 1995, he has taken up writing and given much time to his lifelong interest in folk music, dance and song. He is still an active member of Exeter Morris and Winkleigh Morris. His son and granddaughter live in Sydney.

www.ingramcontent.com/pod-product-compliance
Ingram Content Group UK Ltd.
Pitfield, Milton Keynes, MK11 3LW, UK
UKHW041158161025
464001UK00003B/14